'You have ambitions beyond a remote place like Ballranoch?' Jake had said with an air of disapproval that had touched a nerve.

Cara stared wide-eyed at his back view as his lean figure powered its way round the corner of the drive, and her memory clicked into place like a piece of a jigsaw. Of course she knew exactly who Jake Donahue was! It had been five years ago now, but the brief and memorably unsatisfactory meeting when her father had introduced her to his new locum sprang vividly to her mind. It had been just before she'd left for London and she remembered Jake's raised eyebrows, and his barely disguised sarcasm when she'd told him she was leaving Ballranoch.

But now she was back...

Judy Campbell is from Cheshire. As a teenager she spent a great year at high school in Oregon, USA, as an exchange student. She has worked in a variety of jobs, including teaching young children, being a secretary and running a small family business. Her husband comes from a medical family and one of their three grown-up children is a GP. Any spare time—when she's not writing romantic fiction—is spent playing golf, especially in the Highlands of Scotland.

Recent titles by the same author:

THE BACHELOR DOCTOR

BY

JUDY CAMPBELL

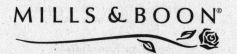

To Leslie and Sondra with many thanks.

First published in Great Britain 2002
Harlequin Mills & Boon Limited,
Eton House, 18-24 Paradise Road, Richmond, Surrey TW9 1SR

© Judy Campbell 2002

ISBN 0 263 83099 3

Set in Times Roman 10½ on 12pt.
03-1002-48944

Printed and bound in Spain
by Litografia Rosés, S.A., Barcelona

CHAPTER ONE

THE wind whipped Cara's hair about her face, stinging her cheeks and making her draw her coat more closely around her. Reaching into her pocket, she brought out the photograph, and for a long moment she looked at it, then savagely tore the paper into small shreds and tossed them over the lookout point. The pieces fluttered like small moths down the valley and she watched their progress against the backdrop of the loch and mountains she had known since childhood.

'Goodbye and good riddance,' she muttered grimly. 'The last day of the old year, thank God! Tomorrow, Cara Mackenzie, is the start of the rest of your life!'

She turned abruptly away and got into the car, flicking a quick, tender look at her little son asleep in his car seat. Long lashes formed an arc on his round cheeks, and a chubby arm was flung out, still holding his battered teddy. Was she doing the best for Dan in leaving London—a job she enjoyed, her friends, her house—and returning to the wilds of Scotland? She shrugged. She'd made the decision now—there was no looking back. It had been a long time, but now she couldn't wait to see her father again and introduce him to little Dan—the grandchild he didn't even know he had.

Driving slowly down the hill, she glanced round at the rolling countryside with the towering mountains in the background, their shapes etched darkly against the cold blue sky, and the town nestling below. It had been five years since she'd been in Ballranoch, unable to come back and admit to anyone—especially her father—that life in London had been anything less than perfect.

And it *was* perfect at first, she reflected sadly. Perfect until…until I found out the truth.

Her knuckles clenched white on the steering-wheel as she turned into the country road where her father lived, and she bit her lip, forcing her mind to concentrate on the present, allowing the old familiar sights to soothe her. She drove past the first of the big houses built on either side—solid Victorian dwellings made of the local mellow stone, standing in quiet and austere dignity at the end of tree-lined drives. It all looked very staid and respectable. Now the sky had changed quite dramatically, as it could in these parts, and the steely blue had darkened as it started to rain heavily.

The sound of thumping music floating above the noise of the rain filtered into the car, and Cara peered curiously down one of the drives—New Year celebrations had obviously started early, she thought with an indulgent smile. Then she drew in her breath and braked sharply as a man suddenly hurtled out of the drive in front of her, waving frantically at her to stop.

'For goodness' sake!' she spluttered, grinding to a halt and looking crossly at the tall figure dressed incongruously in running shorts striding towards her.

'I could have injured you then—what on earth's the matter?' she shouted through the window, certainly not prepared to open the door until she was sure he wasn't going to attack her.

A dripping face appeared before her, water running in rivulets from hair plastered down on his forehead.

'Sorry!' he mouthed through the closed window. 'This is an emergency!'

Cara looked into a pair of deep blue eyes that peered at her through the drips on dark lashes in a tanned face, and felt a slight start of surprise. There was something vaguely familiar about the man's face—surely she'd met him somewhere before? She frowned, trying to kick-start her memory.

'Have you got a mobile phone on you?' he asked loudly, breaking into her thoughts. 'If so, we need to use it!'

Cara opened the window a crack and cut the engine. 'Why? What kind of an emergency is it?' she asked cautiously, her mind still grappling with the elusive thought that she and he were acquainted.

'We need the police and an ambulance here quickly.' His voice was brusque, assured, a man who was used to giving orders and having them carried out. As if reading her mind, he said reassuringly, 'Look, this is for real—a party of youngsters has got out of hand, and one of the girls seems in a bad way.'

Cara blinked. 'Are you a guest?'

A flicker of a smile crossed the man's strong features and made him seem younger, more boyish. 'Not my scene, I'm afraid! I was going on my daily jog down the road when a hysterical young girl came running down the drive and asked me to help her. There's a horde of youngsters holed up in the house—gatecrashers who won't let me in. The girl's friend is in the garden with her and she seems rather ill. It might be a spiked drink, but I'm concerned about her.'

And I thought I was coming to a haven of peace, a little backwater where nothing much happened, thought Cara wryly as she reached into the glove compartment of the car and took out her phone. She stabbed out numbers quickly and flicked a look at the house name on the gatepost.

'Please, send an ambulance and the police to The Glenside House, Spinney Lane, Ballranoch village.' Her voice was crisp. 'There's a party there that's getting out of control, and a young girl who needs urgent medical attention.'

The man nodded as if satisfied with her efficient response. 'Thanks. I'd better get back to her immediately.' He paused for a second and frowned, looking at her more closely. 'Sorry if I startled you. You're not from round here, are you?'

'Originally I was—some time since I've been back, though. Look,' Cara added, 'I ought to come with you. I do happen to be a doctor…'

She flicked a glance to the back of the car. Amazingly Dan was still asleep, exhausted after their long journey and oblivious to the disruption.

The owner of the blue eyes smiled. 'Thanks, but don't worry. I'm a medic, too, and I can see you have your little boy with you. I can cope.'

'He'll be asleep for at least half an hour, and I'd be glad to help—I've got my medical bag with me. I'll park the car just by us so that we can keep an eye on him. The ambulance could take fifteen minutes getting here.'

The man nodded, but looked doubtfully for a moment at the sleeping Dan. 'If you're sure… It would be good to have another opinion and some back-up! I'll meet you at the house. By the way, I'm Jake—Jake Donahue.'

Cara stared wide-eyed at his back view as his lean figure powered its way round the corner of the drive, and her memory clicked into place like a piece of a jigsaw. Of course she knew exactly who Jake Donahue was! It had been five years ago, but the brief and memorably unsatisfactory meeting when her father had introduced her to his new locum sprang vividly to her mind. It had been just before she'd left for London and she remembered Jake's raised eyebrows and his barely disguised sarcasm when she'd told him she was leaving Ballranoch.

'You have ambitions beyond a remote place like Ballranoch?' he'd said with an air of disapproval that had touched a nerve. 'You'll be missed—there's a shortage of doctors here, as you know.' His blue gaze had flicked over her critically. 'Remember, the grass isn't always greener on the other side. You'll just be one of thousands of overworked and under-valued GPs in London, whereas here…'

She remembered the flash of irritation and resentment she'd felt at his implied criticism. Talk about opinionated! Typical of the arrogant sort of male who felt his outlook was the only valid one. He'd only just met her, and he'd had the presumption to assume she was leaving for purely selfish reasons.

She'd cast him a withering look and said coldly, 'My reasons for leaving are my own—I have to live my own life. Anyway, experience is a good thing. I want to see how things work in a city as well as a country practice.'

'I'm sure it will be a good move, career-wise,' he'd replied smoothly.

But, of course, he'd been wrong, she reflected. It had been nothing to do with her career. She'd left because there had been no room for her here any more. She, who'd always loved Ballranoch and the beautiful country around since she'd been a little girl, had suddenly become an outsider, a cuckoo in the nest. Her glamorous new young stepmother had been far too jealous of the close relationship between Cara and her father to want her stepdaughter around for long. The chance she'd needed to get out had come her way, and it had been time to grab it. Not that that had been any of Jake Donahue's business.

'I can always come back…' she'd said defensively.

The sea-blue eyes had looked at her almost mockingly. 'I doubt it. Once the bright lights and excitement of London get to you, Ballranoch will seem very small beer.' Then his expression had softened slightly and he'd held out his hand, gripping hers firmly. 'I'm sorry we haven't had time to get to know each other better. Don't forget about us…and I hope you enjoy your life there.'

That wave of guilt she'd felt then at leaving her father to manage his practice alone came back to her now—Jake Donahue had been quite perceptive. Of course, he hadn't known just what had happened to precipitate her departure—nothing would have persuaded to her stay at that time. Now, with the benefit of hindsight, it was easy enough to see that it had been a huge mistake. She smiled faintly to herself. She'd been on a pretty steep learning curve over the last few years. Had Jake Dohahue changed as much as she had?

The rain was easing, and in the background the steady beat of music had abated somewhat as Cara drew the car up to the side of the house where Jake was kneeling by a young girl. Cara glanced at little Dan, still fast asleep, satisfying herself that she was near enough to keep an eye on him before she leapt out of the car with her medical bag and a rug she'd taken from the back seat.

Through the windows of the house she could see some figures and hear the sound of voices and raucous laughter. The inmates seemed totally oblivious to what was happening outside.

Cara turned her attention to the young girl who was half lying on a garden seat on a verandah at the side of the house. Jake's hand was holding her wrist and he turned round as Cara came up to him.

'This is Anna and her friend Megan,' he said, then dropped his voice slightly. 'I'm concerned about Anna—her pulse is racing and she seems agitated and confused. Megan tells me they both had something to drink, but I'm not sure Anna's symptoms are alcohol-induced. I'd be glad of your input.'

Anna looked round in a dazed fashion, and mumbled something. Behind her another rather plump girl was standing looking totally terrified, twisting her hands together and with tears streaming down her face.

Cara bent down and swept an assessing glance over the young girl, now turning restlessly on the seat and murmuring incomprehensibly. She noted her pallid skin and the light sheen of perspiration on her forehead, and laid the rug over her gently.

'Hope the ambulance isn't long—it's pretty cold out here. She's very, very thin, isn't she?' she remarked quietly to Jake. 'Do you think there's some underlying condition?'

He nodded, frowning. 'She could be anorexic—I'd take a guess her BP's low.'

Quickly taking a sphygmomanometer out of her bag, Cara wound the cuff around the girl's thin arm and watched the gauge as she pumped up the cuff. 'Not too good,' she murmured. 'Eighty over fifty.'

Jake turned to Megan, staring with large apprehensive eyes at her friend. 'You know Anna well, don't you?' His deep voice was kindly but firm, trying to calm the frightened teenager. 'How long has she been like this? It would help if you could describe her symptoms. Take it slowly.'

Jake Donahue may be opinionated, but he's got the right measured approach towards patients, thought Cara. He emanated a calm reliability and she watched, impressed, as Megan took her cue from him. The young girl took a deep breath and swallowed, trying to control herself.

'She…she started being odd about half an hour ago. Said she felt faint. Then she began talking all funny as if she didn't know where she was…said she had stomach-ache.'

'Good, good—that's very helpful. Do you know what it was she had to drink?'

'No. It seemed to be a mixture of things just poured into a bowl—they broke into the drinks cupboard.' Megan's voice started to wobble again and she looked in a stricken way at Jake and Cara. 'I never meant for anything like this to happen—everything's gone wrong.' She brushed a tear away from her eyes and Jake put a hand on her arm.

'Things can be put right,' he said gently. 'Are there any adults here?'

Megan gave a hiccuping sob. 'Grannie and Grandpa went out for the evening, and all these people came and gatecrashed, and they've trashed the house—everything's ruined. They…they trusted me just to have a few friends in, and now… What can I say to them?'

'You mustn't blame yourself,' observed Jake crisply. 'There wasn't much you could do against that horde of hooligans.'

His eyes hardened, and as he turned back to Cara he murmured, 'Her grandparents happen to be patients of ours. I wouldn't have thought they'd have been stupid enough to leave teenagers alone at night—they're supposed to be responsible people. He used to be the local M.P.'

For a second she saw a hint of the tough, opinionated man she'd met five years ago. She shrugged. They were probably elderly and totally out of tune with the behaviour of modern teenagers.

'We can't lay the blame yet—we don't know the whole story,' she observed lightly, then she turned to Megan.

'The police are coming soon and they'll get rid of everybody,' she said kindly, adding in a no-nonsense voice, 'But first it's very important that we know more about Anna—and this is where you can be very helpful. How is she healthwise? What can you tell us about her?'

'Wh-what do you mean?'

'Has she had any pills, drugs of any sort?'

Megan shook her head vehemently. 'No, no—she doesn't do that sort of thing at all.'

'Is she normally healthy, energetic?'

Megan frowned. 'She's diabetic—I know that. She carries things around in her bag for it.'

Jake and Cara gave a quick intake of breath and their eyes met in concern. 'Spontaneous hypoglycaemia!' they both said simultaneously.

'Of course!' Jake thumped his fist into his hand. 'As

you said, she's sweating and apparently confused—both indicators of diabetic distress.'

Megan looked from one to the other, slightly bewildered. 'What do you mean, hypo…whatever? I thought she was drunk.'

Jake shook his head. 'It means,' he said grimly, 'that Anna's system is out of balance. Basically she's suffering from a lack of sugar in the blood. She's probably eaten very little and the insulin she took earlier, coupled with the alcohol, has tipped her into a hypoglycaemic attack.' He looked at Cara. 'Anything in your box of tricks we can help her with?'

Cara nodded, watching Anna closely. 'I think she's slipping into a hypo coma,' she said suddenly, noting the girl's glazed eyes closing. 'I've got a glucometer in my bag that will give a reading of her blood sugar. I'll just take a pinprick.'

They both watched the reading on the small machine and Jake gave a low whistle. 'Pretty frightening reading—under one. She'll need intravenous glucose—50/l00 mils of 50 per cent.'

'What are you doing?' squeaked Megan, as she watched Cara quickly insert a needle into Anna's arm and inject her with a pre-dosed phial of glucose.

'Nothing to worry about. We're just working some magic on Anna—giving her blood some much-needed sugar. Now, watch!'

After a few seconds, Anna blinked drowsily and started to stir, struggling to sit up properly.

'Ah!' said Jake with satisfaction. 'Bingo!'

He and Cara looked at each other in mutual expressions of relief, and for a second Megan forgot her worries about the house and leaned forward in amazement.

'Wow!' she breathed. 'She looks much better already—that's brilliant of you!'

'Wh-what's happened?' Anna looked at Jake and Cara in puzzlement, her voice slightly slurred. 'I feel funny...sort of dizzy.'

'In a minute you'll be back to normal now you've had some glucose,' said Jake, holding her hand comfortingly. 'The ambulance will be here very soon and take you to hospital for a check-up. We need to make sure your diabetes is balanced again—you know how important that is.'

On cue, the sound of an ambulance's siren came wafting over the thudding music, and in a few seconds a police car came speeding up the drive, followed by the ambulance, its blue light still flashing.

In no time at all the drive seemed to be filled with police and paramedics dressed in jackets with large fluorescent bands on them with the words PARAMEDIC or POLICE written on the back.

'Ah, it's Dr Donahue!' said one of them. 'What have you got for us this time, Doc?'

Jake put the paramedics quickly in the picture regarding Anna, and then both he and Cara watched as the young patient was stretchered into the ambulance and driven away.

The music had suddenly stopped and a line of sullen-looking youths and girls were coming out of the house, shepherded like reluctant sheep by several policemen. Megan looked a forlorn and dejected figure standing by Jake's side.

'Don't worry, Megan,' said Cara, going up to her. 'I'll come round tomorrow and see if I can help you clear up the mess. Perhaps you can get friends into help you too. It'll seem a lot better in the morning...'

Megan smiled mournfully at her. 'Thanks very much. I just don't know how I'll face Grannie and Grandpa, though—I was only meant to be having a few friends to stay for hogmanay.'

'Where are you going to stay tonight?' asked Jake. 'I don't think you should be here by yourself.'

'I'll go to my friend's—her parents won't mind me staying over.'

Both doctors were silent for a second, watching the young girl walk in a dejected way down the drive with a police officer to make a statement, then Jake turned to Cara.

'Lucky you happened to be passing. It was a hairy situation and if you hadn't been around, there might have been more to worry about than a trashed house.'

There was an engaging openness about the smile he gave, reflected Cara, giving him a more youthful air than his normally austere expression allowed. In fact, she thought with surprise, flicking a covert glance towards him under her lashes, he was rather a good-looking guy in his way—blue eyes, thick, dark hair and an athletic body—and probably the arrogance to go with it!

She smiled back at him. 'I certainly didn't expect to be thrown into a medical emergency as soon as I arrived back in Ballranoch—I was hoping for a few days' rest!'

Jake frowned slightly, sweeping a critical gaze over her face. 'We haven't met before, by any chance?'

'We have,' she said simply. 'About five years ago.'

He looked at her quizzically. 'Go on—where?'

A faint smile lifted Cara's mouth. 'You were giving me some advice, telling me not to go to London—remember? Said I was letting Ballranoch down by go-

ing off to the Big Smoke and that I would hate it
there!'

Jake nodded. 'Of course! You're Sir Gordon
Mackenzie's daughter, aren't you?' He paused for a
minute, and looked over to Dan in the car. 'I wasn't
aware you had a little boy. Gordon will be thrilled that
you've brought him up for hogmanay.'

Cara's heart fluttered for a second. 'I hope so…
Dan's very excited about seeing him.'

'It's been quite a while since you've been up,' observed Jake. 'You must have a full life in London.
Your career's taken off, has it?'

His words hung in the air, the unspoken criticism
being that her work came before seeing her father.
Cara bit her lip—she was right about the arrogance!

'Ballranoch's a long way from London, and I've
been very busy,' she said tersely.

There was a short silence, and Jake started to dry
his wet hair vigorously with a towel he took out of a
small rucksack, his dark eyes appraising her closely.
'So I was wrong—life's been good to you in London?'

Cara swallowed and thought of the photograph
she'd destroyed, and with it her memories of London.
How this man would love to have been proved right
in his predictions!

'I've made many friends,' she said brightly. 'Had
lots of good times.' She looked curiously at Jake. 'And
you—you're still working around here, then? You
came five years ago as a locum to help my father,
didn't you? I thought you would have moved on from
here—perhaps gone to a less isolated practice with
more facilities.'

Jake's face shadowed for a second and his lips tightened. 'Ballranoch suits me very well.' he said briefly as he stuffed the towel back in the bag.

Cara looked at him with surprise—she seemed to have touched a sensitive nerve there. He looked such a confident man she found it hard to believe there was a chink of vulnerability in that assured manner. She gave an inward shrug. So he had a story to tell in his background. It was none of her business, but she couldn't help being intrigued.

'Do you still help my father, then?' she persisted.

He frowned slightly. 'I would have thought Sir Gordon would have told you I became a partner in the practice a year or two back.'

Cara reddened. 'Perhaps he did mention it—probably slipped my mind.'

'It was getting hard for him, being a single-handed practice, and now I think the workload is too much for him even though I'm here.' He paused, rubbing his thumb on his chin as he looked at her. 'Things haven't been easy for him since his wife…since Angela left, as you probably will have guessed.'

Angela! Hearing that hated name was like having a douche of cold water poured over her, and the blood pounded uncomfortably in Cara's ears. It was hard to escape the fact that her stepmother had been the cause of all the heartbreak in her family, and unconsciously she clenched her fists. Whatever happened now, she was damned if she'd allow that woman to destroy their lives any more.

'I can imagine how my father would feel,' she said tersely. 'I'm afraid she and I never got on very well.'

She made an effort to swing the conversation back to something safer, something that wouldn't tear her heart so much. 'So Ballranoch suits you—and your family?'

'I live in the hills beyond the town—and, yes, I love it around here.'

Cara noticed that he didn't expand on his family commitments. His stern expression softened as he glanced smilingly at Dan in the back of the car. 'It will do Gordon a world of good to see his little grandson. Are you able to stay here for long?'

'Er…I'm not sure.' Cara bent down and put the glucometer back in her bag.

'Dan's father's coming up separately, then?'

Cara flushed and a knife twisted inside her. She would have to get used to this question.

'Dan's father isn't around any more,' she said lightly, as if it had been of no more consequence than him being away on holiday, but her words hung heavy in the air.

'Ah. I see…' Jake nodded. 'I'm sorry.'

She snapped the bag closed and looked quickly at her watch. 'I really must go now—my little boy will be waking up soon and he'll be very hungry. And, of course, I'm dying to see my father.'

Jake smiled. 'Then perhaps I'll see you later at your father's hogmanay party.'

She stared at him in dismay. She'd forgotten about the traditional party, and the thought of being sociable after a long and tiring day wasn't appealing. And how did she know yet that she'd be welcome?

'Perhaps,' she said cautiously.

They walked towards Cara's car together, and he opened her door. 'Thanks again for your help,' he said. 'We made a good emergency team. Perhaps we should start one up—this area's short on emergency cover!'

For a second his eyes locked with Cara's, then he turned and ran back along the drive. Cara smiled as she watched him disappear, an incongruous figure for a winter's afternoon, dressed in running shorts, his shirt soaking wet and outlining the broad muscular shape of his chest. Like a bolt from the blue, a shiver almost like an electric shock crackled through her heart, and the hairs prickled at the back of her neck. Jake Donahue, she suddenly realised, was not only good-looking but emanated a sexual attraction that was rather too compelling!

She stared crossly at herself in the car mirror. Having made a fool of herself once, surely she wouldn't allow herself to react to the first attractive man she'd met since Toby. Men were off limits as far as she was concerned—especially men like film stars with deep blue eyes! She'd been impetuous once before and it had nearly ruined her life. There was no way she was going to get involved in another relationship for a long time—especially with someone who probably had a wife and several children.

Shakily she put the car into gear and drove off towards her father's house. The last thing she wanted at this moment was to have to socialise at her father's party. What she needed more than anything was a time of peace and reflection, to build bridges with her father—not the effort of being sociable with people who were bound to ask questions.

A sigh and a yawn from the back seat alerted her that Dan was stirring and rubbing his eyes sleepily.

'You've been so good, darling,' she soothed as she turned into the tall gates of Glen Shee Manor. 'Soon you'll meet your grandpa, and have a nice drink of milk and some toast soldiers. And you'll be able to play with Buchan, the dog.'

Dan brightened. 'Can I see Grandpa now?' he demanded.

'In a minute,' promised Cara.

Her heart pounded as she parked before the wide front door set in the stone arch with her family's crest carved over the lintel, FAITHFUL AND LOYAL. A faint smile touched her lips. Perhaps it should have been STUBBORN AND UNYIELDING! She wondered if her father would forget the past and give her a loving welcome—or would it be cold indifference? Five years ago she and her father had parted on bitter terms. Now, after all this time and what had happened, she longed more than anything else to be reunited with him.

She drew in a deep breath and stepped forward with her son cuddled into her arms, and pulled the old-fashioned wire bell pull. This was the moment of truth for her and Dan—the next few minutes would determine whether they stayed or left.

There was a jangling noise deep within the house and after a short while the sound of footsteps coming slowly towards them and a dog barking. The door swung open.

The frail, stooping figure of Sir Gordon Mackenzie peered down at Cara and Dan from the steps of the porch and they gazed at each other for a long moment. Then he moved forward and touched her arm tentatively, as if unable to believe his own eyes.

'Cara…Cara—is it really you?' His voice trembled slightly.

Tears welled up in Cara's eyes. How he'd aged! The last time she'd seen him he'd been portly, imposing. Now he looked gaunt, old and very tired.

'Yes, Dad, it's me.' She smiled tremulously and then held up the little boy. 'And this is Dan, your grandson.'

'My…my grandson? My own grandson? But I never knew you had a child.' The old man's voice was a whisper and he looked incredulously at Cara and then Dan. 'How…how old is he?'

'Nearly three.'

'Three!' He put up a hand to touch the little boy's head. At last he said unsteadily, 'You've come to stay for a while, then?'

Cara swallowed a troublesome lump in her throat. 'No, Dad, we've not come to stay for a while. We've come back to Ballranoch—if you'll have us—to live.'

CHAPTER TWO

THE kaleidoscope of white dresses and tartans whirled before Cara in the huge hall and she rubbed the back of her stiff neck. She was very tired, emotionally and physically. As soon as she could, she would slip off to bed. She remembered how the noise of the band and the whoops of the dancers had entranced her as a small child, and what a handsome couple her parents had made, greeting all the guests by the door. Sadly she gazed above the fireplace where the portrait of her beautiful mother had once hung—no prizes for guessing who had taken that down. Angela would never have countenanced any likeness of her predecessor in the house.

She looked across at her father, leaning on his stick, his face sunken and tinged with grey, and felt renewed shock at his present appearance.

'He looks a different person. If only I'd known how frail he was getting, perhaps I would have come back sooner,' she murmured to herself.

She sighed. It was no good, going over what might have been. Her father hadn't stopped her going five years ago—had almost encouraged her to pack her bags, she thought sadly. But things had changed for both of them in those intervening years and each of them would have to learn to forgive and forget. Somehow she felt the first step had been taken. His joy at seeing her and meeting his little grandson had been transparent and she felt a new happiness. Perhaps now bridges could be mended.

In the long talk they'd had before the dance he had brushed aside questions about his health, asking instead all about Dan. His face was alive with interest as he watched his little grandson play with the dog and listened to the child babble away about his toys. Cara hadn't told her father why Toby had left her. It was too painful, and what good would it do to tell her father that part of the story? It would only spoil the evening and his delight in his newly discovered grandchild.

A hand touched her shoulder and a deep voice said, 'I imagine you could do with an injection of something alcoholic. You must be pretty tired after your long journey, to say nothing of your help in the rain this afternoon.'

Cara whipped round to find Jake Donahue standing just behind her in an impeccably cut dinner suit, holding a champagne glass out to her. Her heart gave a sudden lurch. Clothes sat so well on a man like Jake and he looked very different to his afternoon appearance in dripping running shorts and damp hair—and every bit as attractive!

'It was certainly an interesting afternoon—I don't think I've ever treated anyone in the rain in the middle of a rave. I didn't realise Ballranoch had become a centre for gatecrashing parties!'

Jake gave a sardonic smile. 'You thought it was a little backwater village with no excitement? I suppose after London you might think that...'

'I don't lead a very exciting life in London, you know,' she remarked, sipping her drink gratefully. 'Thanks for this—I needed something with a lift. I thought I'd just stay up to see the New Year in then I'll probably crash out. I've missed out on sleep for the past few days, and I should think it shows.'

Jake's eyes travelled slowly over her tall figure, and Cara blushed, suddenly feeling self-consciously aware that the clinging white silk top and black taffeta skirt, which was the only evening wear she had, were probably more revealing than she'd intended!

He looked at her gravely. 'You certainly seem fine to me. And how is your little boy?'

'Dan had a lovely time playing with the dog, but he soon drifted off after he'd had something to eat.'

'Your father seems ecstatic with his grandson—and the fact that you're here.' Jake twirled his glass and looked at her over the rim. 'Said he hadn't known you were coming. Quite a surprise for him!'

'I only decided at the last minute.' Cara put her glass up to her cheek, trying to cool her warm face. 'I thought it would be a nice change for Dan.'

'Sure.' Jake nodded. He looked across at Gordon and then back at Cara. 'And how do you think your father seems?'

'He looks…very frail. I had a shock,' admitted Cara. 'I hadn't expected him to have changed so much.'

'He's certainly gone downhill in the last few months. I suppose you'll be staying until he's had his bypass?'

Cara stared at Jake in disbelief. 'His…his bypass?' she said falteringly. 'He never mentioned it.'

For a moment sadness overwhelmed her—no wonder her father looked so ill. 'I might have guessed he had atherosclerosis,' she murmured. 'His colour's very bad.'

Jake gave her a penetrating look. 'You seem to be in the dark about a lot of things—my partnership, your father's health. Did it never occur to you to come up and see him?'

Tears suddenly prickled at the back of Cara's eyes. 'I know, I know,' she said in a low voice. 'I should have come home before…come and made sure Dad was OK.'

Jake frowned, his voice becoming harsher. 'Couldn't drag yourself away from London—that it?'

There was a short silence and the temperature between them seemed to plunge. Cara flushed angrily. 'You know nothing about it,' she retorted. 'He had who he wanted near him. It was made very clear to me I'd be rocking the boat if I stayed here, and I'd be pleased if you didn't jump to conclusions. There isn't a day since I've been away that I haven't longed to speak to him.'

'Then why didn't you?' asked Jake quietly.

Cara looked at him in angry astonishment for a second, then she brushed a tendril of hair impatiently away from her cheek. 'I don't have to listen to this,' she said brusquely. 'I remember when we met five years ago I thought you were too ready with your own opinions, and my views haven't changed. Your family must find you extremely difficult to live with!'

A gleam of humour lit Jake's eyes. 'That may be so, but it's nothing to do with what we're discussing now.'

'I'm not discussing anything with you,' retorted Cara coldly. 'Now, if you'll excuse me, I'm going to speak to some old friends.'

Jake caught her arm as she turned away, his glance holding hers. 'Wait a moment.' His voice was low but forceful. 'I didn't mean to hurt you, but I've seen your father deteriorate badly in recent months...'

The firm touch of his hand sent a shiver through Cara's body. He was so near, so dominating and demanding, the kind of man who liked things dictated on his terms—and she'd had enough of that. Suddenly she wanted to get away from that penetrating look, that hard male presence.

'You have a nerve,' she snapped. 'I don't know what gives you the right to imply that I've been in any way remiss.'

His grip tightened on her arm, pulling her closer to him. He spoke slowly with deliberation, his blue eyes grim.

'I have a right, Cara, because I admire your father so much. I've worked closely with him for five years now and I know what a wonderful man he is—someone who lives for his patients and treats everyone equally. I only wish I had a father like him. He even put off his bypass operation because he thought he should be here for the practice over the New Year. The best tonic for him would have been to see you.'

Cara's voice was tight. 'I...I regret very much that I've been away so long, but I don't really think it's any of your affair.'

He dropped her arm and said curtly, 'You may be right. Your relationship with your father isn't my business, but his health is. And I think part of the cure is a large dose of t.l.c. from someone I know he loves very much—and that's you.'

Cara was silent. She didn't want to come to blows with her father's partner, and he seemed to have the best interests of her father at heart—she should be grateful for that.

His eyes swept over her troubled face, the slightly parted lips, the wide grey eyes and tumbled auburn hair, and his expression softened.

'Am I forgiven?' he said suddenly.

She stared up at Jake, his strong face bent so near to hers, so close she could see the fringe of dark lashes round those amazing eyes, and the ridiculous thought came to her that the feel of those firm lips on hers would be wonderful, the touch of his cheek against hers sublime. She shook her head angrily. What the hell was she thinking about? Tiredness must have affected her more than she'd thought. She wanted to maintain a good relationship with him for her father's sake, but Jake Donahue was a curmudgeonly man and even thinking about him was absurd.

'I'll…I'll just go and talk to my father for a while,' she said brusquely. 'We've got a lot to catch up on.'

Jake watched Cara's tall slim figure stride across the floor towards her father and cursed softly. Him and his big mouth—no wonder she was upset. How often had he wished he'd bitten back the hasty things he was inclined to say? After all, he had no wish to antagonise the daughter of the man he so admired, but he found it heart-breaking to see a fine man look so broken and sad. He frowned. There was a mystery there. Gordon Mackenzie had never mentioned his daughter in the five years he'd known him, except when asked a direct question. He certainly hadn't mentioned her coming to Ballranoch for hogmanay. Jake smiled slightly. He couldn't help thinking it would be fun to have Cara around for a while—she had a sparky manner that hadn't been cowed by his pointed remarks. He was beginning to realise she could speak her mind as easily as he could!

Cara waved and smiled at old acquaintances as she walked towards her father. It was lovely to be home again, amongst people she'd known and loved since childhood. She'd have to find herself a job, but if Jake was right, one wouldn't be hard to come by, and thank goodness she'd come back before her father's operation.

Gordon Mackenzie was sitting in the large oak chair by the huge fireplace, but stood up as she came towards him, his face beaming happily. That was why Cara thought he was play-acting when quite suddenly and with a terrible groan his expression changed to one of agony. With a choking cry he clutched his chest and sank to the floor, tearing at the collar on his shirt.

She stared at him for a second, unable to take in the reality of the situation. Then it was as if she were moving in slow motion, her legs seeming like lead as she struggled to find the impetus to reach her father's inert body on the floor.

'Dad,' she whispered desperately. 'Dad, what's the matter? Oh, God, hang on there! Don't go! Don't go!'

Even as she reached him, her arms going round him protectively, the thought flashed into her head that little Dan might never get to know his grandfather. Within seconds she felt a strong grip round her shoulders, and she was almost lifted away from the stricken man. Jake stared down at her grimly.

'Pull yourself together, Cara. You've got to be strong for your father now.'

He bent down and loosened Gordon's collar and felt the carotid artery in the stricken man's neck.

'There's still a pulse. Help me prop him up.' Jake turned to the frightened group of people gathered round and said crisply, 'Perhaps you could all go into the dining room.' He flicked a glance at a woman Cara recognised as the practice nurse. 'Sheena, ring for an ambulance immediately.'

Despite her frantic efforts to help him pull her father up against cushions from a chair, Cara was gratefully aware of Jake's ability to take charge and to lower the tense atmosphere.

'You'll be all right, Dad. Don't worry. We're here for you.' She tried to keep her voice calm and reassuring.

Her father gave a slight nod, his face grey, a purple tinge round his mouth. 'The pain,' he gasped, 'Not too good.'

Jake held Gordon's wrist and timed his pulse. 'He's bradycardic—heartbeat well under 60,' he murmured to Cara. He reached in his pocket. 'Here's the key of the drugs cupboard in the surgery—you know where that is, don't you? We need atropine, adrenaline and morphine. Get two of the men here to bring in an oxygen cylinder from the storeroom.'

His instructions were clipped and clear, and they gave Cara something to do rather than stare in terror at her father. She turned and ran towards the small wing in the house that was used as a surgery, her legs feeling like melting jelly. Over and over again she whispered to herself, 'Don't die, Dad, please, don't die. We've got so much to say to each other.'

Jake was still kneeling by her father when Cara returned. He was holding Gordon's hand and talking gently to him, reassuring the man that help was at hand.

'How...how is he?' she whispered, looking fearfully at the grey tired face and sunken eyes.

Jake held her gaze for a moment. 'Be positive,' he murmured. 'Let's get some atropine into him and get his heartbeat up—hopefully we can stabilise him and he won't arrest. I'll try with 1 mg atropine.'

Swiftly he held up the syringe and tested it with a small spray in the air, before injecting it into the man's arm. Then he hooked a mask round the patient's face and opened a valve in the oxygen cylinder one of the guests pushed towards him.

'This should give him help with his breathing,' he remarked in a low voice. 'Cara, did you by any chance pick up a stethoscope there?'

Cara gave him one she'd picked up from the surgery and watched Jake bend forward, listening to her father's heartbeat. Her own heart was beating so rapidly with suspense that she could hardly breathe.

Eventually Jake eased himself back on his heels, and blew out his cheeks with relief. 'Sounding better all the time. I think we've got him on an even keel now.'

Gradually the colour in Gordon's cheeks began to return as his labouring heart started to pump blood more quickly round his body. He opened his eyes and through the mask Cara could see him mouth his thanks to herself and Jake. Her eyes filled with tears. Perhaps this time he'd been saved, almost certainly by Jake's prompt action. She bent down and kissed her father gently on his forehead.

'You'll be all right, Dad,' she whispered. 'And when you've had your bypass you'll be as good as new!'

The night sky was alive with stars, and a bright moon lit up the sprawling shape of St Cuthbert's General

Hospital. A glitter of frost lay over the car park and the windows of the cars still parked there.

Cara drew in a deep breath of the astringent air and closed her eyes. Her father was in safe hands and out of danger in the coronary care unit and it felt as if a heavy weight had been lifted from her shoulders. She turned to Jake who had followed her to the hospital in his car and looked up at his tall figure, a dark, comforting outline beside her.

'I...I don't know how to thank you,' she began. 'If you hadn't been there, I don't think I'd have been quick enough to do something for my father—I just seemed to freeze. It...it's hard to be objective when the patient's a relative.'

'Of course you would have coped,' said Jake briskly. 'It's amazing what you can do if you're forced to.' He looked down at her closely. 'You look a bit shattered. How about a cup of coffee before we go home? The staff canteen's still open across the square here.'

Suddenly Cara felt ravenously hungry, and realised with surprise that she hadn't eaten since a hasty snack on her way up from London. Now the relief of knowing her father was all right made the thought of something—anything—seem imperative.

'You don't suppose they have anything like fish and chips at this hour, do you?' she enquired wistfully. 'I'm starving!'

She could see Jake's mouth lift in a white grin in the dark. 'Why not? That's a great suggestion!'

Cara sat down in the steamy atmosphere of the canteen, busy with various staff grabbing something to eat during the long night shift. She watched as Jake threaded his way back to her with a tray of food. He seemed to know everyone, and she noted with amusement how the women's eyes followed him. Jake Donahue was a striking figure in a crowd, especially dressed as he was in evening dress. She looked down in a self-conscious way at her own dress. Somebody had lent her a thick tweed coat as she'd gone in the ambulance with her father, which at least covered her evening attire.

He put the tray down before her with a grimace. 'St Cuth's haute cuisine isn't all that tempting,' he remarked. 'This is the best I could do. I think it's some sort of fish and an attempt at chips!'

Cara laughed. 'I don't care what it's like—it'll keep me going.'

Jake took a chip from the plate, his eyes regarding her curiously as he bit into it. 'So what will your plans be now? I imagine you'll want to stay and see how your father progresses. You're in general practice in London, aren't you? Will you be able to get cover?'

The noise level in the canteen seemed to rise and for a second Cara was silent, cutting up her fish into meticulous little pieces. It seemed incredible that she had only left London early that morning—surely that was light years away. Now she felt as if she was already immersed in the life of Ballranoch. She looked up and sighed—Jake would have to know sooner or later.

'I might as well tell you. I had left London anyway—given up my job. I...I'm hoping to start again somewhere in this area.'

Jake lifted his eyebrows. 'You have? I thought it was working out OK.'

Cara looked at him defensively. 'It wasn't London itself. It was...circumstances, and I realised that my father might need me. I decided it was a good time to come back.'

'I see,' observed Jake drily, with a slight smile. 'When you decided London was no longer for you, you came running back to Daddy!'

'That's not fair!' Cara's face flushed with anger and she pushed her plate away. 'You really say the most crass things. Perhaps you could wait until you know all the circumstances until you pass judgement!'

Jake lifted his hands in apology. 'You're right! I was out of order there. I know nothing about it. It's just that I feel so much for Gordon—he seemed terribly low when you left five years ago, and then when Angela left him last year it was another blow that he seemed unable to come to terms with.'

Cara bit her lip and looked in silence at the pattern on the Formica tabletop. She flicked a glance at Jake. She doubted whether he knew anything of the dramas that lay behind her flight to London and her subsequent return.

'Angela was the real reason I left home five years ago,' she said quietly. 'She made it very clear that I was in the way. As an only child, my father and I were very close and she was intensely jealous of our relationship. Anyway,' she sighed, 'it was time I made my way in the big world, and I fell for Toby Walsh, the son of a friend of my father's—that's why I went to London.'

It was only part of the story, Cara reflected as she sipped her coffee. It was all she was prepared to tell at the moment.

Jake leaned back in his chair. 'You did the right thing to leave, then. These chances don't come often and, whatever I said to you, one has to grab them.'

There was a tinge of bitterness in his voice and Cara looked at him with surprise. 'You gave me the impression that you thought I was selfish to move away!'

'Perhaps I was biased—the opportunity never arose as far as I was concerned.' His voice was brisk and he gave a slight smile. 'One makes the best of circumstances. I've been incredibly lucky to work with someone like your father in a part of the world I love.'

Perhaps she was reading between the lines, reflected Cara as she picked up her handbag, but there seemed to be a hidden agenda somewhere in Jake's words. She wouldn't pursue it now.

'Thanks for the meal, Jake. I'd better get back, and I'm sure you have a home to go to as well. By the way, I really appreciate the time you've given to help my father.'

'I was pleased to do it,' Jake said quietly. He stood up and smiled at her before saying diffidently, 'This is just a thought, but if you've come up here to work, what about helping me out in the practice? I need someone and your father's mind would be set at rest.'

Cara started to shake her head doubtfully and he put up his hand. 'Before you dismiss it out of hand, give it some consideration—please!' He pointed to a phone booth on the wall of the canteen. 'Just need to call someone before we go. I can't use my mobile here so I'll use that one.'

Cara watched him walk to the phone, wondering vaguely who he was phoning. Then she thought about his suggestion and smiled to herself. Work with Jake Donahue, the most opinionated man she'd met in years? He was a good doctor, no doubt, but could she work with him without completely losing her rag on a regular basis?

'I don't know if working together would be a good idea,' she said lightly when he came back. 'Sparks might fly! I'm not my father, you know. You work so well with him that it might be difficult to make the adjustment to a different person.'

'I'd have to make adjustments anyway,' he observed quietly. 'I think we proved earlier that we can work well as a team. I'd really like you to come on board.'

She shook her head. 'I'm not so sure, Jake. Give me time.' Then she looked up at him mischievously 'And do you usually get what you want?'

He nodded, his normally austere expression softening. 'Nearly always,' he said firmly.

They walked across the quadrangle of the park back to the car, and Cara drew in a deep breath of the crystal air—it was like champagne after the city, a sweet, sharp taste to it. Across the still air came the sound of bells, floating in a joyful cacophony, and the plaintive sound of a lone bagpiper playing somewhere in the hills above them.

'What's that for?' she said wonderingly.

Jake Donahue laughed. 'I'd guess it's the bells ringing in the New Year, Cara Mackenzie. It's just on midnight. Had you forgotten it's hogmanay?'

She looked up at him, her eyes wide with surprise, cheeks pink with the cold night air. 'Of course,' she whispered. 'I'd forgotten—it's been such a frantic night. The start of a new year!'

He smiled down at her, suddenly looking gentler, younger. His broad frame was very close, and one of his arms encircled her shoulders, drawing her near to him. She could see his breath, a white mist, smell the male smell of him, and her heart thumped.

'A guid New Year to you and yours,' he whispered. Then he bent his head to hers and kissed her firmly on her lips. 'I think this is the usual thing to do on a night like this!'

The unexpectedness of it made her gasp, and a flash of excitement flickered through her body. It was a special night after all, and suddenly after the tensions of the evening Cara felt her inhibitions melt away. She relaxed for a second against his hard frame, her arms twining round his neck, pulling him closer to her. Surely, she thought dizzily, one had to celebrate the start of a new year with someone—not just a new year, but a new life!

'And a good New Year to you, Dr Donahue,' she whispered.

Then her body arched against his, responding to the hunger she'd felt for so long now, and her lips parted, tasting for a second the saltiness of his mouth. She closed her eyes as she revelled for the first time for many months in the response of her body to a hard, sexy man. She felt his hands stroke back the tendrils of hair blowing about her face, and his lips fluttering over her face, and then her neck, sending electric thrills round her body. It was as if every erogenous zone in her body was waking up after a long sleep and being galvanised with energy. She leant languorously against this man she hardly knew, allowing herself to luxuriate in the feel of his muscular strength.

Suddenly it wasn't just the bells of the new year ringing out, but a warning bell clanging loudly somewhere in her head. Just what did she think she was doing—practically encouraging a man she'd barely met to make passionate overtures to her in a car park? She shivered, stepping back firmly from his arms and drawing her coat closely about her, overcome with embarrassment. Cara Mackenzie was always in control, wasn't she? Not the sort to fling herself at just anyone. She must be out of her mind. Hadn't she vowed a few weeks ago that she was going to have nothing whatever to do with men for a long long time again?

'We must get back,' she mumbled. 'I can't expect Sheena to watch over Dan any longer. Do you mind?'

His eyes locked with hers for a minute, an unreadable expression in their depths. He opened the car door for her. 'Perhaps that's a good idea,' he murmured.

As they drove away from the hospital Cara took a deep breath, her heart still pounding in overdrive, and watched his strong hands on the wheel. She could imagine them still against her cheek, his lips fluttering in the hollow of her neck, and she acknowledged to herself that the reality was every bit as sweet as she had envisaged earlier when his head had been so close to hers at the dance.

And just where did that leave her if she was to work with him in the practice? she thought wryly. Far too close for comfort in a professional relationship!

CHAPTER THREE

THE small girl looked aggressively up at Cara, her fists doubled up before her like a miniature boxer.

'Don't come near me or I'll hit you!' she shouted. 'I won't let you look in my ear!'

Cara suppressed an urge to smile at the little firebrand, and turned calmly to the child's mother.

'Could you try holding Shona's head again for me while I just peep and see how far the pencil rubber's gone into her ear canal?'

She spoke in a matter-of-fact voice. It was no use getting irritated with the child, although they'd already stretched the appointment well over five minutes while Shona wept and struggled.

Mrs Brown clutched the child to her as if Cara was going to stab her daughter. 'The poor wee pet,' she said mournfully in a hoarse, slow voice. 'She's terrified. You aren't going to hurt her, are you?'

Cara sighed inwardly. Her first morning in the Ballranoch practice had been a full one, dealing with elderly people who had a range of serious complaints to teenagers with bad acne. She didn't feel like battling with too many awkward patients today, however young they were. And Mrs Brown's nervousness was communicating itself to her child.

Cara flicked a curious glance at the woman—large, thin-haired with a thick, pallid complexion. There seemed to be no family resemblance at all to her lively little daughter! Something about the mother's appearance rang a bell at the back of her mind, but it was too elusive to pursue and she turned to the matter in hand. Since she'd had Dan, Cara was even more aware of the terrors that assailed parents when their children were ill, so she was sympathetic to the anxious fears of Mrs Brown—although it was, after all, a very simple procedure.

Perhaps the morning had seemed long because it was her first in a new practice—or perhaps because so much had happened in the two days since the New Year and she felt exhausted. Looking after Dan, going over to see her father in hospital and finally agreeing to help Jake Donahue at the earnest request of her father—they had taken it out of her.

'For my sake, darling,' he'd pleaded. 'There's no one else prepared to work out here at such short notice, and I'd feel so much better if I knew Jake had help. He's a good doctor but even he can't look after everyone.'

She'd allowed herself to be talked into this, she thought wryly. She wanted to do whatever her father said while he was ill, and she'd had enough experience in her inner city London practice to deal confidently with most patients thrown her way. What made her nervous was working in close contact with a complex man whom she'd begun to realise was just a little too attractive for comfort!

For a second her thoughts flashed back to New Year's Eve and the heady feeling of being held against Jake's body, his lips on hers. Her head told her there had been nothing in it—he'd kissed her because it had been hogmanay and she'd responded far too willingly Already she knew her heart was beating to a different tune, and she was afraid that the overwhelming attraction she felt for Jake could lead to nothing but danger…

Abruptly she brought herself back to the curly-headed, pugnacious child in front of her.

'Come on, now, Shona. You're a brave girl, I'm sure, and this certainly won't hurt. Just keep very still.'

Shona started bellowing in reply and Mrs Brown sighed heavily. 'If I hadn't been so tired I'd have been at the school earlier, then she wouldn't have passed the time pushing the pencil rubber in her ear.'

Both mother and daughter tensed as Cara looked into the small ear with her otoscope. 'Ah,' she said with satisfaction, 'it's not gone in very far—I should be able to extract it fairly easily.'

'But surely she'll need an anaesthetic,' objected Mrs Brown fearfully, her dull eyes turning apprehensively to Cara.

'It isn't necessary to put Shona through that. It won't take a second and that's better than going into hospital for a day, isn't it?'

Mrs Brown looked doubtfully at her daughter who responded by burying her head in her mother's shoulder and sobbing.

'If you're sure…' she said, looking with deep suspicion at Cara. 'I don't want you to think I'm being rude, but Dr Mackenzie and Dr Donahue have known Shona since she was born—you don't know her at all. Oh, dear, it's very worrying.'

'It's a very simple procedure. It doesn't matter really that I haven't known Shona since birth, you know,' replied Cara, trying to dampen the impatient tone in her voice.

Mrs Brown started to rock Shona to and fro like a baby. Looking quickly at her watch, Cara realised that this could take a long time to resolve—she didn't want to probe around in the child's ear with an agitated parent trying to keep her still. She pushed the switch on the intercom and spoke to Karen, the large and sensible receptionist.

'I wonder if Dr Donahue or the practice nurse could come through for a second if they're free?'

A few seconds later Jake strode into the room, quickly taking in the scenario of crying child and white-faced mother. Cara flicked a glance towards him and felt her pulse bound uncomfortably on seeing his tall figure dominate the room and amused blue eyes holding hers for a moment. It brought to mind only too vividly their closeness on New Year's Eve.

'Can I help?' he asked pleasantly.

Mrs Brown's pallid face cleared instantly. 'Oh, thank goodness you're here, Dr Donahue. We're having a terrible time with poor Shona and, of course, Dr Cara's completely new to us and doesn't know her as a patient…'

And therefore I don't trust her an inch, translated Cara wryly, her heart still fluttering as she watched Jake walk over to Shona.

'I have every confidence in Dr Cara,' said Jake firmly. 'After all, she is Dr Mackenzie's daughter. Now, what seems to be the problem?'

Cara shot him a grateful glance. 'Shona's managed to get a pencil rubber stuck in her ear,' she said briskly. 'I can get it out very easily, but I wondered if you could hold Shona's head—especially as you know her so well,' she added cunningly.

It took less than ten seconds for Cara to remove the offending object with a pair of tiny toothed forceps.

'There!' she said triumphantly, holding up the rubber, 'That wasn't too bad, was it?'

'You were so brave, darling. I'm going to treat you to a large ice cream,' puffed Mrs Brown as she plodded slowly out of the room. 'Thank you for coming to help Dr Cara out,' she said to Jake, then she disappeared down the corridor.

'Talk about being patronised!' murmured Jake. 'I'm afraid little Shona is rather indulged, being the baby of the family after three boys—and treated like crystal!'

Cara raised her eyes. 'Heaven save me from panicking parents! I'm sorry to have had to drag you in, but I didn't want to pierce darling Shona's eardrum while she wriggled. Her mother told me in no uncertain terms that as a new girl I wasn't up to the job.'

'Better the devil you know,' remarked Jake. 'I'm afraid our patients are notoriously conservative in their views. Of course, you'll know many of them, having lived here all your life.'

'I never worked in the practice, though,' explained Cara. 'I...I was about to, but when I finished my hospital training in Edinburgh things were difficult, as I told you.'

Jake smiled. 'Never mind. You're back now, and I'd just like to say how pleased I am that you're going to help us out.'

'On a temporary basis,' she said quickly. She wasn't going to commit herself to a long stint with this man— it might just turn out to be a huge mistake!

His bright blue eyes held hers for a fraction longer than necessary, as if he knew just what she was thinking, and he gave one of his sudden unexpected grins. 'I'm sure we'll get on fine,' he murmured. 'We have lots to discuss, however. Perhaps we could have a sandwich together in my room at lunchtime. I'd like to fill you in with details of the practice and try and answer any questions you have.'

Cara nodded and started to key Shona's notes into the computer. Suddenly she stopped and looked up at Jake's disappearing back. The elusive thought she'd had about Mrs Brown clicked into place.

'Jake,' she said, stopping him as he walked out of the room. 'Mrs Brown—Shona's mother—she obviously comes to you sometimes, so you know her fairly well?'

'Yes. I don't think I've seen her for some time, though. I noticed she's put on a bit of weight.'

'Well, this might sound completely crazy, but I had a patient in London who might have been her twin sister—same look, same hoarse voice. The patient I had suffered from primary hypothyroidism—I just wondered about Mrs Brown. She said she felt tired and she certainly looked unwell.'

Jake nodded thoughtfully. 'She certainly fills a lot of the criteria—around fifty years old, overweight, female. It's been some time since I've seen her, but she's definitely changed in appearance. You're quite right. We should bring her in for some blood tests—serum TSH and T4 test. Lucky her daughter got something stuck in her ear otherwise it might have gone undetected for some time.' He raised his eyebrows approvingly. 'Good job her new GP was sufficiently on the ball to recognise the symptoms. I'll look up her previous notes and get in touch with her.'

Cara felt a slight glow of satisfaction as she brought up the next patient's notes on her computer. If what she suspected was right and they were able to give her medication, Mrs Brown would feel a different woman very soon. Sometimes, she reflected, being a GP was quite rewarding.

'This was a good idea, Jake. I haven't been down here for many years,' said Cara, looking across the waters of the loch sparkling diamond and blue in the winter sun. Lunchtime had come at last and Jake had steered her firmly out of his room and down the woodland path behind the surgery that led to the loch. It was a cold day, but they both wore thick jackets and the air was astringent and refreshing.

'I thought it would be good to get some fresh air and have our sandwiches out of doors instead of being stuck in the surgery for the whole day. Karen's provided a flask of coffee—we may as well make use of the most beautiful surroundings in the world!'

Cara gazed across to the wide sweep of snow-topped mountains and the small island some way offshore in the middle of the loch. 'That was my island,' she said softly. 'When I was young my father used to row me out there and I had a little den made out of trees—my secret place!'

Jake smiled down at her. 'You'll be able to take Dan there soon. He'll like throwing stones in the water, too, I'll bet.'

'I wonder if Robbie Tulloch, the old gamekeeper, still lives there?' Cara screwed her eyes up to look through the trees on the island. 'He had a dear little cottage on the far side and he used to give me biscuits and milk when I went over.'

'Oh, yes, Robbie's still there, but we don't see him much. He's a patient of the practice, of course.'

He picked up a stone and tossed it into the water,

watching the ripples spread out in circles. 'This is such a wonderful place for a child,' he remarked, a note of wistfulness in his voice. 'Lots of freedom to run about.'

'Were you brought up in the country?' asked Cara, sitting down on an old wooden seat under the trees.

He sat down beside her and offered her a sandwich. 'No, I was a city child—plenty of smog and dirt and not much fun. That's why I appreciate the wilds of the Highlands so much.'

'And that's why you didn't spread your wings for a while and stayed here?'

Jake's face was guarded. 'Something like that. I decided it was best to stay in the area for various reasons. Working for your father seemed to be the right answer.'

His tone didn't invite further questioning and Cara started to undo the top of the thermos.

'Coffee?' she asked briskly, as if she wasn't interested in his background.

Jake nodded and leant forward in his seat, clasping the hot cup in his hands. 'Perhaps I ought to tell you something about the way we work here then you'll get an inkling of what you've let yourself in for.'

'Is it a big practice?' asked Cara. 'In London we were a two-handed partnership with about six thousand patients between us.'

Jake shook his head. 'Not quite that big, but huge in area, as you can imagine. As you know, St Cuthbert's is the local hospital and it has a good A and E and surgical service, but all neurological cases have to go further afield. Can be tricky if a climber has fallen on the hills and hit his head. By the way,' he said turning to her, 'do you have walking boots and good all-weather gear?'

'Not really. Why—will I need them?'

'Most certainly,' Jake said, a rare smile touching his lips. 'We're the back-up emergency team if things go wrong—and you'll be amazed how often that happens!'

Cara was silent for a second. She'd certainly done the odd emergency case in London when doctors had been needed in road traffic accidents, but she hadn't envisaged herself tramping over the hills and climbing mountains to rescue people!

'Does it put you off?' Jake raised his eyebrows humorously at her. 'I think you'd find it invigorating—and you wouldn't be on your own!'

Cara gave a slight gulp. That might be part of the problem—being on her own on a windswept mountain with Jake Donahue might be a bit too exciting! 'I...I don't know anything about climbing,' she protested.

'You'll be fine,' he said. But she wasn't convinced.

'We do have an arrangement with a practice about twelve miles away to do some late on-call visits, and we have a minor injuries unit at the surgery once a week for patients who can't get to the hospital easily. There's an occasional bus that wends its way to Ballranoch from outlying districts.'

Cara nodded. It would be a very different working life to the one she'd led in London where her patients had lived in close proximity to the medical centre and an agency had done late night calls—that was for sure!

Jake stood up and stretched. 'Ah, well, back to the grindstone. By the way, I looked up Mrs Brown's notes and the last time she came to see me was about a menstrual disorder, which of course could be an indicator of hypothyroidism, although she had no other symptoms. We tried her with cyclical progesterone and she seemed to improve.' He smiled at her. 'Very good detective work if I may say so!'

The wind blew icily down the loch and Cara pulled up the collar of her coat. 'All in a day's work,' she said modestly.

'How was your father when you last visited?' Jake asked as he gathered up the lunch things.

'He's stable and they're thinking of doing the bypass in another week if he maintains good progress. I may take Dan in with me soon—it might give Dad a boost to see him.'

'I'm sure it will.' He flicked a quick glance at Cara. 'Had your father never seen him before?'

Cara flung the dregs of her coffee into the undergrowth and sighed. 'My father never even knew he existed until New Year's Eve—that's why he never mentioned him to you.'

'Then you came back at the right time,' said Jake quietly. He held out his hand to Cara and pulled her up from her seat. 'I see you decided to use your maiden name—Mackenzie. What's your married name?'

'Toby and I never married—we never got round to it.'

She watched an osprey circle high in the sky over the loch and sighed. She'd wanted to marry, had hoped against hope that Toby would one day commit himself to her, especially when Dan had arrived. She smiled wryly to herself. The baby's arrival had made Toby even more remote, if anything. And now, she thought bleakly, it was as if she had never known the man, never spent over four years with him...

She was brought back to earth by the sharpness in Jake's voice. 'That's a great pity, isn't it? No father for Dan. Or is he still around?'

Cara bit her lip. She wanted to tell Jake to mind his own business, to forget the hurt that Toby had caused her—but what good would keeping it dark do?

'Toby has no interest in his son. In fact, he has so little interest he's gone to live abroad.' She looked at Jake defensively. 'You don't approve, then—you think I should have married someone like that?'

Jake shrugged. 'I just think for the child's sake it's more secure. I know marriage seems to be going out of fashion but, speaking for myself, there's no way I'd have a family without being fully committed to the mother of my children. Are you sure you couldn't have made it up with him—at least kept in touch with him for Dan's sake?'

Make up with Toby? Cara almost laughed. 'After what that man did to me and Dan,' she said grimly, 'I never want to set eyes on him again.'

Jake shook his head rather sadly as they started to walk up the path, and Cara looked curiously at him. 'You've very conventional views—some people feel just as committed to each other when they aren't married as those who are. You've been living too long in the wilds!'

He raise a sardonic eyebrow. 'Maybe I'm out of touch, but it seems a shame to have a baby without the father being around.'

A flash of irritation went through Cara—he certainly could be pompous at times! 'Be real, Jake,' she snapped crossly. 'You know accidents do happen. Sometimes human beings get it wrong—we're not machines!'

There was a hint of scorn in his look. 'Come on, Cara, surely as a doctor you could have foreseen a little ''accident''!'

The cheek of the man! Cara felt her blood pressure starting to rise alarmingly. She stopped walking and stared at him, her eyes sparkling with rage, spitting out her words. 'How dare you say that? I don't regard Dan as an accident—he's the best thing that's ever happened to me!'

She turned abruptly away from Jake, her pulse racing with anger. How could she work with this boorish man who seemed to enjoy insulting her at every turn? He might be one of the most drop-dead-gorgeous men she'd ever seen but it didn't prevent him from shooting his mouth off!

He touched her shoulder and pulled her round to face him. 'Don't take it like that, Cara,' he said gravely.

'Look,' she rejoined hotly, 'you're entitled to your own opinions—just keep them to yourself, that's all!'

His grip tightened on her shoulder. 'Of course your son is everything to you, it's just, well, I see a lot of girls left to carry the can when their boyfriends go off. I hate to see someone like you and Dan hurt.'

Those deep blue eyes burnt into her. Jake meant what he'd said and, to be honest, he had a point. Toby had left her to fend for herself with a baby, and it had been hard. She was determined that Dan would never suffer for it, but the sad truth was that he would probably never know his father—and she was happy for it to be that way. She took a deep breath, trying to calm her anger with Jake, but the sting of the truth in what he'd said didn't make his outspokenness any easier to take.

She looked up at him defiantly. 'I'd better be quite candid,' she said brusquely. 'My father wants me to work with you and I don't want to upset him at the moment. But if you keep pontificating on the way I run my life, I shan't be staying!'

He dropped his hands from her shoulders abruptly and raised a sardonic eyebrow. 'That sounds like a threat,' he remarked.

'Well, I feel very strongly about it!'

'I have no intention of telling you how to live,' he said stiffly. His voice hardened. 'All I do know is that in the unlikely event of my meeting the right person and deciding to have a child, I'll make darned sure I'm married first.'

For a second a most curious feeling of jealousy filled Cara's heart. The girl Jake ended up with would be a lucky one, she thought. He would take his responsibilities very seriously and would never abandon his wife and children. She gave him an appraising look. He was a mixture, this man—confident, handsome, and yet there was something aloof about him, a touch of the loner in some ways.

She shrugged. 'You have an idealised view of marriage. It doesn't always lead to happiness—as I know from my father's experience.'

Jake looked at her stubbornly. 'It's not something to be jumped into, I agree—but where children are concerned, I believe marriage is imperative.'

'And, as a responsible person, would you like children?' Cara asked coldly.

'Perhaps.' His voice was noncommittal, careful to give nothing away. 'The time has to be right—and, of course, one's got to meet the right person.'

Cara raised her eyebrows. 'And that's not happened yet?'

Suddenly that stern demeanour relaxed somewhat, and a slight smile touched his lips. 'There aren't many single girls around Ballranoch who want an impoverished doctor in their lives!'

The temperature between them seemed to lower a few degrees as he looked down at her with a hint of amusement in his eyes, and Cara felt a treacherous tingle of excitement hit her. She tensed as he brushed a strand of hair away from her cheek.

'You'd probably be the first to admit that any relationship is a gamble after your experience,' he said with more gentleness in his tone. 'But perhaps if you'd married Toby you'd still be together—right?'

Cara moved away from him and opened the door to the surgery. She wasn't ready to forgive Jake's outburst concerning Dan just yet.

'I doubt that very much,' she said coldly. 'And as you know nothing about Toby's relationship with me, I don't know how you can make that assumption!'

What Toby had done to her—and indirectly to her father—could never be forgiven, but it wasn't any of Jake's business. She marched quickly to her room, her feet making any indignant tattoo on the wooden floor.

Only one more patient to see before she could go and collect Dan from his nursery and hear all about his day. Cara stretched luxuriously. That was one very good thing—her lovely son seemed to have taken like a duck to water to the nursery that her father's daily, Annie Shaw, had recommended to her. Annie had also asked if she could stay in 'the big house', as she called it, whilst Gordon was in hospital. She was a young, lively woman who wanted to get away from living at home with her mother for a while, and she was longing to help look after Dan. At least, thought Cara gratefully, her worries about child care for Dan had been alleviated.

She sighed and stared distractedly at the PC screen in front of her. It was her relationship with Jake that worried her. Just how easy was it going to be to work closely with someone who manifestly disapproved that she was a single mother—that somehow she should have 'known better'? Angrily she pressed the switch that activated the screen in the waiting room telling patients that she was ready to see them. It shouldn't matter what he thought of her, she told herself—she should just get on with her job. But it did matter. Jake was beginning to get under her skin and she couldn't forget his cutting comments.

She brought up her next patient's notes on the screen and tried to put the annoying Dr Donahue out of her mind. Then she leaned forward with more interest and raised her eyebrows—the address of the next patient was the house where the rave had been two afternoons ago!

She was surprised to see that the woman who came in was middle-aged. She'd got the impression that she would be elderly—after all, Megan, her granddaughter, was at least fifteen. Mrs Forbes was smart and well groomed with streaked golden hair, and she was wearing a beautiful camel-coloured cashmere coat. She looked the kind of confident woman who knew what suited her and had her life in order.

Cara's mind flicked back to Jake's rather scathing comments about leaving teenagers alone in the house on New Year's Eve—perhaps he'd had a point. Mrs

Forbes certainly wasn't the doddery, out-of-touch pensioner Cara had imagined, and she wondered if the afternoon of the party was something to do with the woman's visit.

'Ah, Mrs Forbes, do sit down,' she said, indicating the seat in front of her desk. 'How can I help?'

Mrs Forbes gave a bright smile—too bright perhaps—and clasped her hands tightly in front of her.

'I...I don't really know if it's a problem I should bother you with,' she began hesitatingly. 'The fact is...' Her voice faltered and she put a hand up to her forehead, scrabbling about in her handbag to find a handkerchief which she pressed for a second to her eyes. 'The fact is, doctor, I've been a complete and utter fool!'

Cara waited as the woman stared at her, her lips trembling as if trying to psych herself up to tell Cara what was wrong. At last she blurted out breathlessly, 'I don't know why I'm telling you this, but I've got to unload it somehow. It's been a terrible few days. I...I'm Dr Donahue's patient really, but I couldn't discuss this with him...with someone I know.'

'Take your time,' said Cara gently. Wryly she thought that some patients objected to seeing a new doctor in the practice, whilst others positively welcomed it!

Mrs Forbes swallowed and bit her lip. 'You probably heard of the damage done to our house outside the village when some yobs came and trashed the house...'

'I did happen to be there. Dr Donahue and I were helping a young diabetic girl in the garden.'

'Then you'll know how stupid we were to leave my granddaughter, Megan, and her friend by themselves.

I can't forgive myself, and I can only say that I was so worried about…personal matters that I felt I had to get out for the night. Megan is so good I couldn't imagine anything awful happening.'

'What things were you worried about?'

There was a short silence as the woman gathered her resources. She gave a deep breath.

'I'm afraid I might be pregnant!'

'How old are you, Mrs Forbes?' Cara asked gently.

'I'm nearly fifty. You wouldn't think it would be possible to get pregnant at my age, would you?'

Cara smiled. 'If you're still ovulating, it's perfectly possible. How many weeks do you think you are?'

'I don't know—could be quite a few. I just never dreamed this could happen to me!' Suddenly Mrs Forbes's face crumpled and she put her hands over her face as she sobbed her heart out. Cara got out of her chair and put her arm comfortingly on the woman's shoulder.

'Come on now, Mrs Forbes, let's just make sure you are pregnant before you get upset. There are other conditions that have similar symptoms to being pregnant, you know. At your age the menopause is probably starting to kick in.'

Mrs Forbes dried her eyes. 'But I thought one had hot flushes and other symptoms—I haven't had anything like that.'

'Not necessarily.'

'I haven't had a period for some time…I was having them fairly regularly up to three months ago.'

'I take it a baby wouldn't be welcome, then? Have you mentioned this to your husband?'

The woman gave a mirthless laugh. 'I certainly haven't! Anyway, it…it's not as simple as me just having a baby.' She sighed. 'A baby would have been so welcome many years ago—I only had one child and I'd have loved another. No...the trouble is...' Her voice sank to a whisper. 'I've been seeing someone else. It was just a bit of fun, you know, nothing serious. My husband is a good deal older than I am and hates going out now.' She twisted the handkerchief round in her hands, and her voice started to rise. 'I just got tired of sitting around all the time, doing nothing, but it would ruin everything if he found out. I don't know what would happen to me!'

'You think he would leave you?'

'My husband is well thought of in the community—he's an ex-MP, you know, and he wouldn't welcome being made a fool of if this were to come out.'

Talk about selfish, thought Cara. No thought of the hurt she'd cause her husband, only what the consequences might be for her if she was found out. She got up briskly. It wasn't for her to make moral judgements.

'First of all, let's establish if you really are pregnant—I take it you haven't done a pregnancy test? When you've given me a specimen of urine I'd like to examine you.'

Margery Forbes looked anxiously at Cara as she put the strip of paper in the specimen a few minutes later. After a few seconds Cara looked up. 'This result is negative—I think you could be worrying unnecessarily. Let me just examine you—it's possible to be fairly certain of pregnancy by the state of the cervix.'

After the examination, Cara drew off her protective gloves and threw them in the bin, then washed her hands. 'I don't think you have anything to worry about Mrs Forbes—I'm practically sure that you're not pregnant. Just to make absolutely certain, I'll take some blood for a test on your hormone levels. It may indicate what I suspect—that you've started the menopause.'

'Thank God!' said the woman, closing her eyes and lying back on the couch. 'I felt I was living a nightmare!'

'This doesn't mean you can't get pregnant,' warned Cara as she dried her hands. 'Until your periods have stopped for a year, you should protect yourself.'

Mrs Forbes got off the couch and smoothed down her immaculate tweed skirt. 'There won't be any need,' she said forcefully. 'I've learnt my lesson, and…well, I shall try and be more sensible.'

A familiar scenario, thought Cara bitterly as Mrs Forbes left the room. A younger woman marries an older man and then gets bored. She knew it only too well, for wasn't that her father's sad little story? Mrs Forbes seemed absorbed with herself and on New Year's Eve she'd put her own needs before that of her granddaughter. It could have ended disastrously with the death of a child.

Cara gave a little shrug of wonder at the secret lives of her patients and switched off her computer. She suddenly realised that she was dying for a restoring cup of tea and, when she'd put Dan to bed, a soak in a hot bath. That was why when there was a knock at the door she was tempted to call out, Go away!

'Come in,' she said a trifle wearily.

Jake looked round the door, his face apologetic. 'I know it's late and you're really tired, but I need a big favour. Everyone's gone home and my car's finally run out of petrol—I had an unscheduled emergency call out in the hills. Could you just drop me off at the garage on your way to pick up Dan from his nursery, and I'll get a gallon to keep me going?'

Cara stared coldly at him—she hadn't forgotten his remarks about 'accidental' babies. If he thinks he can just slip back to being Mr Nice Guy, he's got another think coming, she told herself fiercely.

'No trouble,' she said tersely.

As he settled himself into the car, Jake turned to Cara, his strong face made more angular by the shadows of the streetlamps.

'I'm glad of the chance to see you by yourself,' he said in a low voice. 'I want to say something to you—something important. I should have kept my big mouth shut earlier. I must have hurt you very much, and I wouldn't do that for the world. I...I do sometimes jump into things with both feet, I know.'

'You've noticed, have you?' Cara's voice was heavily sarcastic.

'I've been told often enough by my sister,' he said wryly. 'I apologise.'

Cara stared at him and put the key in the ignition. 'And that's supposed to make everything all right, is it?'

He put his hands on her shoulders and turned her towards him. 'I hope it helps a little. Look, I want our working relationship to be a success, and I know it can be. Please, allow me to take you out for a meal to try and make up for my crassness. I really want to make amends.'

His voice was low and coaxing, and his arm was slung round the back of her seat, making him far too close for comfort. Suddenly the space in the car seemed to contract and the atmosphere was just a little too intimate. Cara felt Jake's warm breath on her cheek and she was hardly surprised when his hand turned her head to his so that his dark-flecked eyes held hers.

She swallowed. This was too reminiscent of the other night when they'd kissed so ardently. Even thinking of that made her senses tingle, and an urgent longing came over her to repeat the experience. She shifted nervously away from him in her seat.

'You don't have to take me out,' she said in a tight little voice. 'Just keep your thoughts to yourself.'

His finger traced a line under her chin. 'Believe me, I'll try. As you said, I've been too long in the wilds and I've forgotten how to behave.'

There was something bleak in that statement, something that spoke of loneliness and isolation—even chances missed. What was it in Jake's past that had led to his reserved and blunt manner? Cara knew that under that stern exterior lurked a humorous and warm personality—she'd encountered it on New Year's Eve. There had to be an explanation for the façade he presented. All at once her anger with Jake seemed to dissipate like seeds in the wind.

'It would be nice to go out for a meal,' she said lightly as she turned the key in the ignition. 'But, remember, I've got a hearty appetite!'

'I'll keep you to that,' he murmured.

When they reached the garage, Jake got out of the car and watched as Cara drove off, hunching his shoulders against the bitter wind. It always had been a failure of his, to speak first and think afterwards. Perhaps it was the result of a harsh upbringing where people spoke their minds and didn't wrap things up in glossy words, and the circumstances he found himself in now. The irony was, he reflected sadly, that he seemed hell-bent on hurting Cara Mackenzie—the sort of girl he'd been looking for all his life, sparky, humorous and far too beautiful to be let down by wastrels such as Toby.

He dug his hands into his pockets and bunched his fists. It was a pipe dream to wish that he and Cara could get together anyway. It could never happen, not with things as they were at home. There was no way he could make the commitment to Cara that she deserved, and for that reason he had to keep his distance.

'Forget about it, Jake Donahue,' he muttered as he turned towards the garage. 'It's never going to happen.'

CHAPTER FOUR

CARA screwed her eyes up against the bright light and stared at the two figures floating high in the sky and drifting their way over the loch from the heights of Ballranoch Ridge high above her. Against the clear blue winter backdrop they looked like oddly shaped birds with one huge wing.

'Look, Dan,' she said, one arm round the stout little body of her son, the other pointing up to the sky. 'See up there? Those are men with special harnesses on with wings like birds—it's called paragliding.'

Dan looked up at them for a minute, and then said very seriously. 'I think I'd like to do that, Mummy.'

Cara laughed. 'When you're quite grown up—and then you'll have to have lessons, because it could be very dangerous otherwise.'

'Why? Why dangerous?'

'You could fall to the ground if you didn't do it properly and hurt yourself.'

The little boy nodded, then turned his attention to Buchan who was rushing up and down the lochside, barking at some ducks that had ventured near the shore.

'Come on, Buchan!' he shouted. 'Come and play football with me!'

He ran down the shingly shore, kicking a small ball along, and Buchan raced in front of him.

This is better than being in the town, thought Cara, watching her son with pride as he shrieked with laughter trying to beat Buchan in getting to the ball first. Dan didn't seem to have any hang-ups about being a one-parent child, she reflected—he was full of confidence and fun. There would come a time, she supposed, when he would compare himself with other children and see them with fathers. That might bring problems, but until then he was a carefree little boy who was enjoying his third birthday.

'Let's go fishing now!' he cried, running up to Cara, his cheeks rosy red.

'I've no fishing rod, love,' said Cara. 'Perhaps we'll go to the village and see if they've got one, and then we'll go to the little farm for a birthday treat.'

'Yes!' shouted the little boy joyously.

The crunch of feet on the shingle made Cara turn round. Jake's tall figure was wending his way towards them with a box in his hands. Cara's heartbeat increased slightly. Since his apology to her after her first day at the practice, he had been courteous and friendly but definitely not over-friendly. It was as if he was keeping a distance between them, not wanting to get too close after he'd restored things between them. The subject of the meal out hadn't been mentioned again.

He squatted down before Dan and smiled at him. 'I believe it's someone's birthday round here,' he remarked, placing the box on the ground. 'This is for that birthday person.'

Dan jumped up and down excitedly, his big brown eyes sparkling, his arms up in the air. 'That's *me*! I'm the birthday person!'

'Then you'd better open it!' Jake's eyes met Cara's over the child's head. 'I hope it meets with your approval,' he said.

Cara smiled. If Jake was trying to make amends, it

was a kind way to do it. 'How did you know it was Dan's birthday?' she asked, reflecting how relaxed Jake was with the child. His stern demeanour had melted into a happy, teasing expression, and she could tell from the way Dan reacted to him that children would adore him.

Jake laughed. 'It wasn't difficult. I was just leaving the surgery after the baby clinic, and I could hardly get out of the hallway for the amount of opened parcels strewn about!'

'That's because of my father,' said Cara ruefully. 'He rang up the local toy shop from the hospital and instructed them to send most of their toys here! We're going later this afternoon to see him with Dan's birthday cake for a quick little tea party.'

Dan was busy tearing the paper from the present Jake had brought. He peered into the package and then with a whoop of delight pulled out a fishing net. 'That's what I wanted! Now I can go fishing! Thanks!'

He ran off down to the water's edge and trailed the net energetically around for a few seconds. Then he came running back. 'There's no fish there,' he said sadly. 'They won't come to the net.'

'Perhaps I could take you to the little harbour up the coast,' said Jake. 'There's some rock pools there that probably have lots of creatures in them.'

Dan looked at Cara. 'Yes, let's do that!' He shouted. Then he grabbed Jake by his hand and started pulling him back towards the house. 'Let's go now!'

'That's what I call enthusiasm.' Jake smiled.

Cara regarded the two figures in front of her, so disparate in size, and a wistful ache started in her throat. This was what it should be like for Dan always—a father playing with him, taking an interest in him, enjoying his simple little pleasures, just like Jake was doing now. She saw Dan lift his face up to Jake and say something to him, and watched Jake throw back his head and laugh heartily. A flicker of surprise went through her. So he could let himself go! But it took a child to do it.

They went to the harbour, a few miles away by the mouth of the loch, and caught tiny little crabs and limpets from the rocks. Dan was in seventh heaven, wading round the pools in his little wellingtons and watching the fishing smacks set off for the sea beyond the harbour. Then Jake introduced them to a patient of his, an elderly fisherman with a huge beard, who took them for a short sail in a little dinghy so that Dan could say he'd been in a boat.

It was quite magical for the little boy. 'Can we do this again?' he said wistfully to Cara as they wended their way back to the car. 'Jake says he'd like to—he says it's the best day he's ever had!'

Jake caught Cara's eye over the child's head. 'That's quite true,' he said, 'I think we ought to make a habit of it!'

Something in the way he looked made Cara blush and she looked quickly away. Today it had seemed that Dan had been part of a proper family—and it felt wonderful.

'Thanks, Jake,' she said. 'You've made it a happy day for Dan.' She paused for a second and added softly, 'And for me as well.'

Her father looked better, thought Cara with relief a little later. He was propped up in his hospital bed in a small single room off the main ward. The blue tinge round his lips had gone and he was smiling delightedly at his grandson.

'I thought you'd like that Lego,' he said with satisfaction. 'I used to love that sort of thing when I was little—used to make very complicated things out of bricks.'

The little boy leaned confidingly against the bed, his bright eyes looking up at his newly found grandfather. 'When you come home, Grandpa,' he said, 'I'll make you somefing very special—just for you.'

Gordon didn't speak for a moment, just stroked Dan's head.

'You think you'll have the bypass next week?' Cara asked her father as she cut a small piece of birthday cake for him.

'I'd like to get it over—fed up with lying in this hospital. Sooner I get back to work, the better!'

Cara frowned. 'We've had this out before, Dad. Jake and I are managing very well together. You must have a long rest—most people your age have retired!'

Gordon growled. 'I'm not hanging up my clogs yet, my girl!' He looked questioningly at his daughter. 'Think you and Jake can get along all right for the time being? I know he can be pretty outspoken sometimes, but if you don't let it bother you he's a good man.'

Cara smiled. 'He certainly says what he thinks. In my estimation he's been living in the hills too long. I assume he lives by himself—a crusty old bachelor!'

'He lives with his sister—I know that much,' said her father. 'I've never seen her—they keep themselves very much to themselves. I get the impression she's very reclusive.' He sighed. 'I'm fond of Jake. I don't think his life has been all that easy, but he's been a tower of strength when things have been bad.'

Cara looked quickly at her father. 'You mean when Angela left?' she said bluntly, taking a leaf out of Jake's candid approach.

Gordon nodded. 'I did feel low—but that was mostly, my darling, because I longed to see you. And when you did come, why, what a wonderful bonus! I found I had a little grandson. And I tell you what— he's made me feel a whole lot younger!'

He looked lovingly at Dan, now building a road over the floor with his bricks.

'Well, you're not worry at all about the practice,' said Cara firmly as she started gathering up Dan's toys. 'As I said, Jake and I have got things running smoothly.'

'Aye, he's a good doctor.' Gordon nodded. He looked at his daughter under bushy brows. 'And not bad-looking either!'

Cara turned her head away quickly. She didn't want her father to see the tell-tale blush that showed she agreed with him.

It had been a long day for Dan, and as soon as his head hit the pillow his eyes closed. Cara went to the window and looked out at the black sky, pierced with twinkling stars and a pale moon that lit up the loch waters and showed the dark shape of the island. A wind had got up, blowing in from the sea and the waves on the loch were choppy. The trees were starting to sway as the weather worsened.

Cara started to draw the curtains, then stopped, peering more closely out into the night. Surely that was a light she could see flickering across from the island? Perhaps it was Robbie Tulloch, doing his rounds to see that all was well. She looked again, more intently. It didn't look like the bobbing light of someone walking—it looked much more like a signal. Yes! There it was again—three short flashes, followed by three longer ones and then a further three short. Didn't that stand for S.O.S.?

Quickly she ran downstairs and picked up the telephone, stabbing out Jake's number. In a few seconds she heard his deep, familiar voice answering.

'Jake, I've just been looking across to the island. I think Robbie Tulloch could be in trouble. There's a light winking in what looks like the S.O.S. sequence. I can't understand why he hasn't phoned us. Shall I get in touch with the police?'

A wry laugh came from the other end. 'They've got to come from twenty miles away—the man could be dead before then! I'll come straight over and use the boat to get to him and phone for emergency help on the way.'

'I'll meet you by the little jetty, then. I'll pull the rowing boat from the boathouse so that it's ready to use.'

Pulling on an old windcheater of her father's, she called out to Annie that there was an emergency and she'd be back soon. Cara ran out to the loch, stumbling over the thick shingle. The weather was worsening rapidly, clouds starting to obscure the moon.

Annie stood in the doorway, watching her go. 'Take care, Cara,' she shouted out. 'The waters on the loch are treacherous when it's like this!'

Fumbling with the thick rope that secured the old rowing boat, Cara managed to unhook it and, pushing with the oars, steer it out of the boathouse. It was years since she'd done this, she reflected, puffing hard as she pulled against the water. She'd allowed herself to get flabby and out of shape. There had been a time when rowing this boat had been easy—now she was ashamed of how unfit she'd become.

I'll start a new training regime tomorrow, she vowed as she drove the boat onto the shingle and leapt out breathlessly, pulling the boat close to the shore.

Cara looked across to the island. The light still blinked on and off and there was no doubt in her mind that it was a cry for help. Gradually, as the weather closed in, the light became a feeble little pinprick. Cara looked worriedly back at the road in front of the house—she hoped Jake didn't live too far up in the hills.

To her relief she saw the lights of a car turn into the drive and in a few minutes Jake appeared, a rucksack on his back and well geared up for the weather in boots and oilskins.

'I'll get across there as quickly as I can,' he said. 'Probably the lines are down, so I'll signal back to you—three flashes will mean I need more help, two flashes I can manage OK.'

Cara looked at Jake pugnaciously, her hands on her hips. 'Don't be ridiculous—you can't go on your own. Suppose Robbie's collapsed? It'll need two of us to carry him back to the boat, and one to support him and one to row. I'm coming with you!'

'No way!' growled Jake. 'I'm not letting you put yourself at risk unnecessarily..'

For an answer, Cara leapt into the rowing boat. 'Come on!' she snapped. 'We're wasting valuable time here. I've rowed across here hundreds of times— I know the best route. You row, I'll do the navigating!'

He gripped the side of the boat. 'Don't be a darned fool, Cara. You've got a little boy to think of.'

Cara's eyes were flinty as she stood in the rocking boat. 'Let me worry about that… For heaven's sake, hurry up or I'll go by myself!'

The waves were whipping up alarmingly, and the moon dodged in and out of the clouds, giving an adequate but unsustained light. Cara could still see the large tree which she'd always used as a landmark when rowing towards the island and gradually they made the small beach. Jake leapt out of the boat and hauled it up the shore until Cara could jump out on the sandy ground.

'I see the light now,' called Cara above the wind. 'Let's go!'

A few minutes later they found Robbie at the edge of a small copse. He was standing up, still signalling with his torch.

'Robbie!' gasped Cara. 'What's happened? Are you all right?'

'Ah—at last!' he grunted, turning towards them. 'I was hoping you'd see my signal. There's nothing wrong with me—it's this young man we've got to worry about. He's called Seth, and he's got himself caught in the trees. Brought down the telephone lines, too.'

He pointed up into the largest tree of the group, swinging his torch so the beam spotlighted the figure of a man hanging almost upside down from a branch. Lines and straps of a harness were draped round him, and the flapping shape of multicoloured parachute fabric fluttered above his head.

Jake whistled. 'What the hell happened?'

'He's a paraglider,' said Cara. 'I saw them flying

above me this morning. He must have been there for some time.'

The man groaned, and Jake started to climb up a nearby tree. 'I'll just try and see what damage he's done. Hang on there, Seth, we're going to help you,' he added, trying to shout above the noise of the wind.

There was a sudden scream of pain from the man as the wind gusted against the branches and swung his hapless body to and fro. 'Be quick!' he said in a feeble voice that they could only just hear. 'I think I've done something to my back.'

Cara and Robbie craned their necks to watch as Jake leant dangerously across to the stricken man, casting the light of his torch over his body. Cara heard him talking to Seth, trying to calm him and reassure him that something would be done.

After a few minutes Jake swung himself down. 'Not looking too good,' he told the others. 'He's bleeding heavily from his leg—he's probably lost quite a bit of blood, and his back's at an awkward angle. Some branches have caught his head so I don't think he'll have whiplash but, like it or not, we've got to try and get him down and stop the bleeding. The good thing is that his leg's at an angle so that's reducing the blood flow slightly.'

'What about his back? It'll be very difficult to keep his head and spine still.'

'Have you got any canes, Robbie?' asked Jake. 'We'll make a support for his back from them, and if you've got anything like a board we could strap him to that when he's on the ground—keep him rigid.'

'Then we've got to get him off this island somehow once he's down from the tree. I don't fancy taking him across in that boat.' said Cara, filled with dismay at the thought of doing more damage to Seth.

Jake was already punching out numbers on his mobile. 'We need urgent help,' Cara heard him say in his calm clear voice. 'We're on the island on Ballranoch Loch. A man's fallen into the trees whilst paragliding. Get the air ambulance here pronto—his injuries make a boat rescue inappropriate.' He looked at Robbie. 'Where can they land?'

'There's a good spot by the cottage—quite an open area. I'll go and light a small beacon by it after I've got the canes for you.'

Jake relayed this information down the phone and put it back in his inner pocket. 'Come on,' he said grimly to Cara. 'Let's get Seth out of this mess. Robbie, get back here as soon as you can—and bring a rope as well as the canes and board. The helicopter's coming from another rescue in the hills, so it could be a while.'

Cara scouted round the area of the tree and found some small branches, and from Jake's bag they found scissors to cut some of the parachute lines hanging from the tree. She started to make a sort of brace for Seth by weaving the branches together and fixing them firmly with the cord.

Cautiously Jake began to climb the tree Seth was imprisoned in until he was nearly touching him.

'Give me a bit of information, Seth,' he said clearly. 'Can you move your hands and feet? Have you any specific pain?'

The man's voice was muffled and faint, but he managed to whisper, 'I think I can move them, but it's hard to breathe and I've got a pain in my side.'

'Can you feel me touch your legs?'

'Yes… Oh, hell, my chest… Every time the wind blows me it hurts my chest.'

'Hang on there, mate, Robbie's come back with some equipment. We'll get you down. Be strong.'

And now for the hard part, thought Cara grimly, watching as Jake contorted himself in the branches to fix the home-made brace she'd made to Seth's neck. She could hear Jake panting with the effort of keeping his balance and moving his arms at the same time, and felt a flash of admiration at the way he was risking his life for this unknown man. There had been no question of holding back, waiting for the air ambulance.

'Robbie,' he shouted, 'can you come up on the other side of me? I need your help to take Seth's weight when I cut the harness that's holding him. I'll then try and make a cradle with that parachute fabric and we'll lower him to the ground.'

He makes it sound relatively easy, thought Cara wryly. She wondered what she could do, apart from try and break the fall of three heavy men if they crashed down! She looked behind her. Robbie had wrenched an old door from a broken-down shed near his cottage and dragged it near. It would be a good thing to bind Seth's body to and keep his spine still while they waited for the air ambulance.

There was a spattering of rain through the trees and in the distance a rumble of thunder.

'That's all we need,' grunted Jake as he helped to haul Robbie up with him in the fork of a big branch by Seth's hanging body. 'We'll have to get him down somehow. On balance I think the priority is to stop the bleeding rather than worry about the possibility of spinal damage—anyway, this wind is swinging him alarmingly.'

The two men worked feverishly round the man, cutting some of the lines and cords and gradually weaving a kind of hammock with the parachute. Carefully they placed it round Seth's body and drew one end up towards them. At last Seth's body was almost parallel to the ground instead of nearly upside down.

'I'm cutting the rope that's holding him now,' called Jake. 'Robbie and I will lower him as gently as we can towards you, Cara. Get ready to steady him and slow his landing.'

It was a painfully slow business. Jake and Robbie strained every muscle to keep the man's passage as smooth as possible, but every so often his body would catch the trunk or a branch of the tree and he would groan.

'Nearly there!' shouted Cara encouragingly. She put her arms up to balance Seth's body and take some of the weight the men were supporting. Eventually he landed on the door she'd positioned under him.

'You're down now, Seth,' she said calmly. 'I want to look at this gash on your leg and the men can secure you in a fixed position to this door Robbie found. We've got to keep you as still as possible.'

Seth didn't reply. His eyes were closed and by the light of the lamp Cara could see he was deathly pale. She looked up as Jake and Robbie clambered down, both breathing heavily.

'I should think his BP's pretty low,' she said to Jake. 'We've got to stop this bleed—there may be internal injuries as well, causing blood loss.' She started to form a pad of some gauze bandaging she'd found in Jake's medical bag and pressed it firmly to the site of the wound, pushing her rolled-up jacket under the man's leg to elevate it slightly. Jake and Robbie finished strapping Seth to the door as best as they could.

Jake leant back on his heels, and puffed out his cheeks in relief. 'Now, let's pray that the air ambulance gets here soon.'

Almost as he said the words, the rumble of an engine was heard overhead. Robbie scrambled to his feet.

'I'll go to the clearing,' he said. 'They should see it easily with the downward beams they've got, and I've got quite a good fire blazing. I'll direct them to you.'

The clatter of the helicopter became deafening, and the leaves stirred in the branches.

Seth's eyes opened. 'What's happened?' he whispered. 'Where the hell am I?'

'You're about to go on a pleasure trip,' said Jake with a grin. 'I hope it's not as exciting as your paragliding today. Don't you remember landing in the tree earlier?'

Seth smiled weakly. 'Yes, I do—not very softly either.' He screwed his eyes up and looked at Jake. 'Did you get me down?'

'It took three of us,' said Jake. 'I wouldn't like to do it again!'

'Thanks… I'm very grateful.' Seth's voice faded away again.

'His pulse is pretty low,' murmured Cara, holding Seth's wrist between her fingers. 'He'll need blood substitute and cross-matching in the helicopter before they reach the hospital. Whatever other injuries he's sustained, he's probably cracked some ribs—his breathing's very shallow.'

They both looked up as two men in green and yellow suits came running through the undergrowth with Robbie, his old lungs wheezing with the effort.

'Here's your passenger,' said Jake.

'Sorry we took so long—we were just in the process of taking a pregnant mum from a farm in the hills to St Cuthbert's. They couldn't get past the snow on the hillside.'

'He'll need some haemacel and, of course, oxygen.' Jake informed them briskly.

One of the men looked doubtfully at the door on which the man lay. 'Think we'd better keep him on that—don't want to fling him around too much. We'll put a proper neck brace on, I think—good though that contraption is that you've got on him now!'

'It's a work of art!' protested Cara, as she watched the paramedics slip on the brace.

'OK, then, let's go!' yelled one of the men.

The improvised stretcher was lifted with great care, the men moving as quickly as they could through the woods with Robbie guiding them.

Cara and Jake followed the paramedics to where the helicopter had landed, like some giant insect in the clearing. They watched as a platform was lowered from the door and Seth's makeshift stretcher was loaded gently onto it.

'Good luck, Seth,' yelled Cara, going up to the platform. 'We'll come and see you in hospital!'

Then they watched as the machine lifted off the ground and clattered away, lights flashing, into the distance.

'That was a rum do,' said Robbie as they strolled over to his cottage. 'If I hadn't been taking the dogs round the island I doubt if I'd have seen him till the morning.' He shook his head in wonderment. 'I always said something like this would happen, the way they hurl themselves off the mountainside like that—and I was right! Now, come in and have a wee dram—do you good after all that!'

The walk back to the boat was dark—even with the torch it was hard to see the path. The weather had deteriorated even more, large waves washing the shore of the loch and the wind howling eerily through the trees.

'Do you think this is wise?' Jake remarked doubtfully. 'Perhaps we should go back and beg a bed from Robbie for the night.'

'It'll be all right—it's not very far across from here. I'm really exhausted after all that exertion, and I don't fancy kipping down on one of Robbie's truckle beds!'

Jake shrugged. 'OK. Let's go!'

They'd reached the water's edge now and expected to see the boat still moored to the little stump of wood they'd hooked the rope to.

Jake was the first to speak. 'I thought we left it here,' he murmured. 'Where the hell is it?'

Cara clutched his arm and pointed to the shore opposite. 'Look,' she shrieked. 'The boat's slipped its moorings—it's halfway back!'

Sure enough, fast bobbing away from them could be discerned the shape of the rowing boat. Almost at the same time another tremendous crack of thunder reverberated across the mountains and as if a bucket had been upturned on them, a downpour of tropical dimensions started to lash down.

Cara spun round and buried her head in Jake's shoulder. 'I hate thunder,' she moaned. 'Let's get back to Robbie's—the thought of the truckle bed sounds much better now!'

Jake stood stock still. 'I hate to tell you this, Cara,' he said, 'but I've dropped the torch. If we can't find it, I doubt if we can find our way back to Robbie's!'

'What? I don't believe it! We can't spend all night in the pelting rain. What are we going to do?' Cara's face was almost comical in its expression as she looked in a horrified way up at Jake's pale face.

'We'll have to scrabble down in the shelter of those bushes—can't go under a tree in a thunderstorm. We'll wait for the storm to pass. I'll ring Annie on my mobile and let her know we're all right.'

Cara was horrified. 'This is ridiculous!' Another crack of thunder sent her flying again against Jake. 'Oh, no…let's go, then!'

She grabbed Jake's hand tightly in the almost total blackness of the night, and together they stumbled towards the low bushes that fringed the shore. Jake pulled her down behind one of them. 'If we lie low here we won't come to any harm from lightning, and it's surprisingly dry.'

'I'm cold.' Cara shivered. 'I forgot to pick up my coat when I put it under Seth's leg. It's probably in the helicopter now.'

'Here—take this.' Jake pulled off his oilskin and wrapped it so that it almost enveloped them both. 'Best to keep close together—we don't want to get hypothermia.'

She relaxed against him, suddenly exhausted from the tension of the evening. 'Thank heavens we got Seth out safely,' she murmured.

For answer he pulled her slightly more towards him.

'I know—it was a very near thing. Another half-hour and it might have been too late.'

Cara shivered again—but this time it wasn't from the cold, it was for a very different reason. Every nerve in her body suddenly seemed on fire, she was so close to Jake, his body hard against hers, the male smell of him assailing her nostrils. Slowly she felt his arms wrap round her, binding her helplessly hip to hip with him, felt his head bury itself in her neck.

'Is that comfortable?' Jake's voice was soft, slightly slurred, and she could feel his lips move against her skin as he spoke.

'Y-yes,' she whispered breathlessly. 'It's all right. I feel quite warm now.'

'I know you do—you're radiating heat.' His hands moved to her neck and then her hair, and all at once she was lying under him on the ground, his strong body straddling hers.

'Jake…' Cara's voice was a feeble protest, and she heard him give a low chuckle.

'I'm trying to keep you dry,' he murmured.

Then suddenly his mouth was covering her face with kisses, his lips fluttering down to the hollow in her neck. 'I'm sorry,' he whispered. 'I can't damn well help it. Your hair shouldn't smell so sweet, you shouldn't feel so soft and beautiful. It's driving me mad…'

She struggled against him, then fell back as she felt his fingers slipping their way under her jumper, caressing her breasts with the lightest of touches. Her mind whirled with a thousand contradictory messages—she wanted him to make love to her, this complex man who seemed so aloof in many ways. There was a passion inside him that she realised would be difficult to quench—but where would it end? In broken dreams and lost love like it had been with Toby?

A warning shiver went through her. 'Jake,' she whispered. 'Should we be doing this? I…I don't know if this is right.'

'It feels very right to me,' he murmured, lowering his mouth to hers again and teasing her lips apart. She felt her insides liquefy with longing and her own arms wound round his neck and pulled him close against her, giving in to the insistent clamour of her own desire.

'Now, what could be wrong about this?' she heard him murmur.

As if in a dream she felt his hands gently unzip her jumper down the front and peel back her T-shirt, then his head bent down and he was covering her with butterfly kisses that made her arch her back against him with desire. His hands, so expert in their caresses, explored her body with a tantalisingly gentle touch. How easy it would be to give in to her needs—to let Jake take her completely. She lay back in a kind of dream, allowing him to cover her with soft, insistent touches that made every erogenous zone in her body scream with pleasure.

The flash of lightning that split the sky above the loch made her jerk back with surprise, and a jolt of common sense ran through her mind. Was it entirely wise to get this heavy with a man she had known so short a time and who undoubtedly carried baggage from the past with him?

A niggling little voice said inside her, Why complicate your life again when you've just managed to get it straight? Surely you've had enough heartache to last you several years?

She was a fool to respond so easily to this man she hardly knew, to lead him on when she'd been betrayed by Toby whom she'd thought she'd known so well.

'No, no, Jake…not yet,' she gasped, firmly wriggling away from him. He knelt back, sensing her unwillingness. 'I'm sorry,' she whispered.

She leant back against the stump of a tree and closed her eyes. Suddenly, as it did so often, a horrible picture from the past flashed into her mind. She was opening the door of the flat in London, holding onto Dan's hand. For a second the picture was hazy. She couldn't quite understand what was happening before her—two figures were writhing together on the carpet. Then with sickening clarity she realised that one of them was Toby, doing to a woman what he had done to Cara so lovingly before… Although Cara was shielding Dan from the scene, he was turning his head up towards her. 'Mummy, what's Daddy doing?' he was saying in his soft baby voice. The picture faded. Somehow it would be very difficult to trust a man again.

She opened her eyes and saw in the half-light that Jake was watching her.

'Sorry,' he murmured. 'I got a little carried away there—perhaps it was Robbie's whisky!'

Cara kept her voice light and inconsequential—best not to make this too big a deal. She smiled up at him. 'You and me both! You haven't phoned Annie yet—perhaps we'd better do that. She'll send someone over for us in another boat now the storm seems to be passing. Remember, I'm on call in the morning!'

There was a short silence, only broken by the light sound of the rain as it pattered on the ground, and Jake suppressed a sigh as he took out his mobile. Why the hell had he allowed himself to give into his longing to hold Cara, when common sense had told him to keep well away? It must have been relief at the end of a stressful evening—how else to explain the way he'd given in so easily to his feelings?

Cara had had her heart broken once, although Jake couldn't understand how anyone could have betrayed someone as beautiful, feisty and fun as she was and leave her to bring up that dear little boy by herself. But his longing for Cara must be firmly suppressed. How could a poor boy from the slums of Glasgow hope to form a relationship with a girl from a privileged and wealthy background and, even more pertinent, how could he expect a young woman who already had a child to bring up take on the weighty responsibility he had to carry? It was too much to ask of her.

'You're right,' he said, getting up and brushing the leaves from his clothes. 'Best to try and get home before we forget the time entirely!'

Cara watched as he phoned Annie, his strong face a white blur in the darkness. She'd seen a different side of Jake Donahue this evening—a glimpse of a warm, humorous and passionate personality too often submerged by a remote outer shell. Shock waves of desire still rippled through her body, but she had been right to have stopped their love-making—she needed more time for her scars to heal. And wouldn't it be wrong to start a steamy affair with a colleague, even one as good-looking as Jake? She smiled to herself— it was good that they had kept it light-hearted. Whatever had happened, she was sure they could laugh about it the next day. She knew that after this evening things would be more relaxed between them.

CHAPTER FIVE

CARA covered a yawn with her hand and tried to look alert. She'd been on call since seven a.m. that morning and had had to cover any emergency visits until the surgery started at eight-thirty. All in all, after the adventures of the night before, she hadn't had much sleep. She'd had an emergency call from far out in the countryside at seven-thirty—a distressed farmer whose wife had bad abdominal pains. Cara had decided the woman needed hospitalisation for further investigation. Now, sitting at a morning meeting with Jake and the Ballranoch Area Director of Technology, she felt as if she'd already done a day's work.

They were discussing the networking of the computer systems of all the GP practices in the area and the local hospital. Cara glanced across at Jake, leaning forward earnestly to put his case to Bernard Lewis. She noticed rough scratches on his face where the branches had caught him during the rescue—had it been only a few hours ago that they had been entwined in an intimate embrace, and that firm mouth had been pressed to hers? She touched her lips with her finger as if she could still feel the tingle from his kiss, and closed her eyes as she remembered again how closely he had held her.

She looked forward to dealing with a more approachable, relaxed Jake now, but so far he'd barely looked at her—just nodded a brief greeting.

'We need to be able to e-mail referrals to consultants at St Cuthbert's much more quickly,' Jake was saying. 'Rapid access is especially important for cancer patients—it's important that they're seen by a specialist as soon as possible.'

Bernard nodded. 'That shouldn't be difficult. I'll set up a meeting for this to be discussed next month at the hospital.'

'It would be good if we could book patients directly in for their surgery,' suggested Cara. 'At the moment we don't know for ages how long someone will have to wait. It would help forward planning enormously.'

Jake nodded approvingly. 'Good idea!' He stood up and shook Bernard's hand. 'We'll be hearing from you soon, then, regarding the agenda.'

Bernard snapped his briefcase shut and smiled at them both. 'Fine! By the way, I hear there were a few dramas on the island last night. You were heroes, I believe, rescuing a man who'd fallen into a tree—it's the talk of the town!'

Cara felt the colour rise in her cheeks and she flicked a look across to Jake, but he seemed unperturbed and answered in a level voice, 'Quite exciting really—when you go paragliding, make sure you land in a soft spot and not when it's dark and there's a storm blowing!'

'Sounds like a fun evening.' Bernard laughed as he left the room.

Cara's eyes locked with Jake's for a moment, expecting him to say something droll, but he merely started gathering up his papers and walked to the door.

'That went fairly well,' he observed briskly. 'By the way, thanks for all you did last night. It was a great effort.' Then he went out.

Cara gazed dumbfounded after him. Was that it?

Was that all the reference he would make to what had gone on after they'd rescued Seth—not even a humorous comment? She shook her head in disbelief. Surely he couldn't be that cold—the moment of passion they'd shared together couldn't mean that little to him. Why the sudden change from affection to complete chill-out?

Cara frowned and sat down for a moment in her office, as she gathered her thoughts together. She hadn't imagined that Jake was the sort of man who'd forget entirely about their little episode last night! Gloomily she chewed the end of her pen. The sad fact was that she couldn't get it out of her mind—every tingling nerve and electric response came back to her when she thought of their bodies twined together and his demanding lips on hers… OK, so she had brought their love-making to an abrupt end last night—she wasn't ready yet to commit herself after Toby's betrayal of her—but surely it had been worth a mention?

The buzz of the intercom on the desk made her jump, then Karen's voice floated over the room.

'Hello, Cara, I've a journalist, Pete Marbury, here from the local paper. He wants a word with you and Jake about the accident you attended last night—have you a minute some time?'

'I could see him now if you want. I don't know how Jake's fixed.'

'He says he can give him a few minutes—they'll come into your room.'

Pete Marbury had the look of an eager young puppy, thought Cara as he bounced into the room after Jake.

'I only wish I'd managed to get across during the

rescue operations,' he lamented. 'We could have got some great pictures. Was it difficult to get the man down from the tree?'

Jake nodded. 'It certainly was. We had to try and keep his body as rigid as possible in case he had injured his back badly.'

'And had he?' asked Pete, pencil poised above notebook.

'He'd sustained a serious injury and will need an operation to stabilise it. Good job we got him to specialist help within the golden hour.'

'The ''golden hour''?' repeated Pete, looking puzzled.

'If the patient can get to hospital where all the latest technology is available to him within an hour of injury or, say, heart attack, it's been found that the chances of survival are increased by a huge percentage,' explained Cara. 'That's why it's called the golden hour—and that's why the air ambulance is so invaluable.'

'By the way,' Jake said, turning to Cara, 'I rang St Cuth's and apparently after a CAT scan they discovered Seth had a compression fracture of his thoracic l2 vertebra—he's lucky not to have any neurological deficit.'

'What does that mean?' asked Pete, scribbling furiously.

'It means he wasn't far off being paralysed—a small piece of one of his vertebrae is lodged very near his spinal cord.'

'Wow!' exclaimed the young reporter, impressed. 'Sounds like you guys did a good job. It can't have been easy, keeping him still and getting him down to the ground.'

A slight smile crossed Jake's lips. 'Dr Mackenzie here did a marvellous job with an improvised brace, and Robbie Tulloch was a wonderful help—without him the helicopter that took Seth to hospital couldn't have landed.'

'Well, we can thank you docs for that—I think I can make a good story out of all this!'

Cara suppressed a sudden fit of laughter. It was nothing to the story he'd have got if they'd told him what had happened after the rescue!

Pete looked from one doctor to the other, a hopeful gleam in his eye, and as if he had just read Cara's thoughts he said, 'Just on the human interest side, I don't suppose you two are romantically involved? It would just add a bit of punch to the story if you did happen to be!'

'We're professionals who work together in the same practice,' said Jake frostily. 'I'm afraid we can't oblige your readers with personal details! You wanted a story of the rescue—you've got it!' he added tersely.

'OK! See you soon!' Completely unabashed, Pete Marbury left the room, giving a cheery wink to Cara as he left.

'You were a bit hard on that young reporter,' commented Cara.

'Cheeky young blighter.' Jake frowned, gazing after him. 'I told him all he needed to know.'

'You didn't tell him everything, though, did you?' Cara leant against the desk and folded her arms. 'Tell me, Jake, have you forgotten the little scenario after Seth was rescued? Did it mean so little to you?'

Jake looked startled. 'You didn't want me to tell the whole world?'

'No, but I thought you might have mentioned it to

me this morning—any normal person would at least have made reference to the fact that we enjoyed ourselves last night. Have you got a hang-up about that?'

He looked at her angrily. 'Of course I haven't! And, of course, it meant something to me…'

'I'm not asking for lifelong commitment,' said Cara. 'I'm just saying you must be a pretty cold fish to have put it so well to the back of your mind!'

He strode over to her and caught her arm, pulling her towards him, his voice harsh. 'I'm not one to blab to all and sundry about my private life—and, no, I hadn't forgotten about it.' Then his tone softened and his blue eyes became less flinty. 'The last thing I want is for you to think I'm taking you for granted…far from it.' His gaze raked over her face, taking in her wide grey eyes and tip-tilted nose, lingering for a second on her parted lips. 'The truth is, I've had time to think about last night, and I don't want to lead you on, Cara. There's no use you getting involved with a man like me. It wouldn't be fair.'

Cara frowned. What did he mean by a man like him? She was convinced he wasn't a womaniser. He seemed responsible. Just what secret did he have in his background that made him unsuitable for getting involved with and that had made him want to warn her off? She looked at him shrewdly. It probably had nothing to do with him at all. More likely it was because he didn't want to become involved with a girl like her—someone who had a child and hadn't *bothered* to get married! She was sure that deep down Jake had a problem with that—hadn't he said as much before?

She shrugged. 'OK, it's no big deal. We'll just have to keep off Robbie's whisky in future!'

He nodded gravely. 'Best put it behind us, eh? Keep things professional.' He went out of the room.

Absently Cara drew a heart on the pad in front of her. Keep things professional indeed! He hadn't worried about that last night! He was a funny, old-fashioned guy, and it was odd how much of himself Jake kept quiet about. Even after five years, her father seemed to know little of his family or background. Well, she thought, unconsciously jutting out her chin with determination, she would find out about Jake's mysterious background sooner or later!

She stabbed at the keys on the computer and brought up details of her first patient of the day on the screen. She felt in her bones it was going to be a long day. She was bound to come into contact with Jake and how difficult would that be? She pushed the thoughts of awkward encounters with him to the back of her mind and started work.

The afternoon surgery was coming to a close. Cara stretched with relief. Later she'd go to the Ballranoch Leisure Centre and make her first effort at getting fit, which she'd vowed to do the previous night. Her final patient was Megan Forbes, whom she'd last seen on the lawn of her grandparents' house on the afternoon of New Year's Eve. It seemed as if the whole Forbes family was coming to her for medical advice!

The young girl sat down in front of her, boldly made up with her big blue eyes outlined, with black lines and purple lids. Her lips were a startling vermilion colour and moved vigorously as she chewed a large wad of chewing gum. Her plump little body was squeezed into the shortest miniskirt Cara imagined Ballranoch had ever seen! She looked a different girl to the one Cara had seen at the party. Then she'd been very distressed—now she seemed quite bouncy, almost defiant.

'I wanted to see you, Doctor, 'cos you…you seemed so nice at hogmanay when we had that awful time. You won't tell anyone I've come, will you?'

'Of course not,' said Cara gravely. She smiled kindly at Megan. 'Are things back to normal now? Did you get into much trouble?'

Megan frowned. 'Grandma's hardly mentioned it— she's been very quiet. Normally she'd throw a real wobbly—it's my grandfather whose been awful. There's a real atmosphere because he's not stopped going on about it and he and Grandma keep shouting at each other. He blames her for making him go out that night and all the trouble it led to.'

She took a deep breath. 'That's why I've decided to go away for a while. I've been living with them because my parents are abroad at the moment, but I'm old enough to live by myself. I want a job—I want to get away from Ballranoch!'

A sentiment that rang close to home, thought Cara a shade sadly. 'What do you want to do—and where do you want to do it?'

'I'm going to be a model,' explained Megan. 'I've read loads of magazine articles, and that's what I've decided I'll be.'

'But, Megan,' said Cara in dismay, 'surely you have to have training—and I see from your notes you're barely sixteen. Your grandparents won't be too happy that you want to leave home.'

Wryly she reflected that Margery Forbes was going to have more to worry about than her husband finding out about her affair if her granddaughter disappeared!

Megan shook her head impatiently. 'They won't mind. I'm just a nuisance and responsibility to them—they're always saying how worried they are about me!'

'Now, that's not right. They love you very much, I'm sure. Please, talk it over with them before you make any rash decisions.'

'I may do…but I don't see how they can complain. After all, my grandmother did modelling—she's always on about it.' She shrugged as if dismissing further discussion on the matter.

'I see,' sighed Cara. 'Is there anything else?'

Megan nodded. 'The thing is, I wonder if you'd look at my back? I've got these horrible moles all over the place, and if I'm going to be a model I can't have any blemishes. I've read that moles can become cancerous—especially if you sunbathe a lot.'

Cara nodded. 'It's true that the incidence of skin cancer has increased. I don't know if it's because people sunbathe more, or if the sun's rays are hotter! Let me look at them under a strong light.'

Megan took off her top, and Cara looked at the three moles on her upper back through a magnifying glass. After examining them carefully, she put the glass away. 'I don't think you've anything to worry about, Megan,' she said. 'To me, one looks like a seborrhoeic wart, and the other two like benign skin growths, little skin tags really—all of them harmless.'

'Are you sure?' asked Megan, looking immensely relieved.

'Pretty sure, but because of the increase in skin cancer generally and to ease our minds, I think it's best we remove them and send them away for biopsy—

that's a careful examination under a microscope just to see their composition.'

'Would there be a scar? If I'm going to do photographic work I mustn't have marks on my back.'

'Only very faint, and that would go in time—you could easily use make-up to disguise them. I could do them now for you, if you like.'

Megan looked apprehensive. 'Not in hospital? Won't it hurt?'

'Not at all. I'll anaesthetise your skin with a local anaesthetic, and put a few stitches in when I've cut the moles out. You'd have to come back in a few days for the nurse to take out the stitches. I don't want to use dissolving ones because they can sometimes form thicker scars on the skin's surface.'

'OK,' agreed Megan, transferring her chewing gum to a piece of paper in her pocket.

As Cara carefully cut out the moles she felt a wave of apprehension go over her. Just how many of the girl's dreams were going to shatter in the cut-throat world of modelling?

'Where are you thinking of doing your modelling, Megan?' she asked, putting a temporary protective pad over the little cuts.

'Oh, London, I think,' said the girl. 'That's where you get all the breaks, you know. I'm going to get my portfolio done soon—lots of photos. Then you send them up to agents or magazines.' She sounded so confident, as if getting into the modelling business was the easiest thing in the world.

'But surely it's best to have training?'

'Not really—I've heard of dozens of people who've made it big without any trouble.'

Cara nodded bleakly. She just hoped London would

have a happier outcome for poor little Megan than it had for her! 'Promise me, Megan, that you'll not do anything without telling your grandparents—after all, they've had one shock with the party. Keep on good terms with them, whatever you do!'

Megan smiled, a sudden sweet smile. 'Don't worry Dr Mackenzie—I'll discuss it with them if you like.'

'Good girl! Come back and see me next week and we'll take out the stitches—and then perhaps you'll tell me what you've decided.'

As she keyed in Megan's notes and finished labelling the specimens for analysis, Cara grinned to herself. Who said coming up to Scotland would be dull and slow? The scenario being played out in the Forbeses' household was a fascinating one, and as for slow—last night's adventure would last her for some time!

Karen brought in some coffee for her. 'It's really snowing hard out there,' she said cheerfully. 'It'll be thick by tomorrow and all the skiers will be coming up at the weekend.'

'Are you a skier, Karen?' asked Cara, remembering happy days as a child when her father had taken her on the nursery slopes. It had been a sport very much in its infancy in Ballranoch then.

'Oh, yes, I love it. Perhaps you'd come with me one day? Ian, my husband, helps to run the ski-lift. It's extra money for him—but, my, it can get very cold up there!'

The phone began ringing in the surgery and Karen ran back to answer it. A few seconds later she came back to Cara looking rather worried.

'That was the nursery your little boy attends. Apparently, Dan's had a fall from their little slide and seems to have hurt his arm. He was pretending to be a paraglider.'

Cara stared at Karen in dismay. 'Oh, no! I told him to wait until he was grownup for that!'

She peered through the blinds of her room at the darkness outside—thick snowflakes were whirling through the air.

'He would do it when the weather's at its worst,' she added gloomily. 'I'll go now and see what's happened. Dan will probably need an X-ray.'

Jake appeared at the doorway. 'Sorry to butt in, but I just wondered if printouts of any of my e-mails had landed on your desk—I'm waiting for the results of some blood tests and biopsies.'

'There's quite a few there that may have got mixed up. I haven't had time to look at them yet.'

'I'll look for you,' said Karen. 'Cara's just heard her little boy's had an accident at his nursery.'

Jake looked up sharply. 'It's snowing heavily. You can't go on your own—especially in your small car. I'll take you. I've got chains for my wheels if we get stuck.'

'No, no, thanks, I'll be quite all right.' Cara started putting her coat on hastily. The last thing she wanted was to sit in the close confines of a car with Jake Donahue, making polite conversation. 'It may be that he's just strained his wrist and needs nothing more than a bandage.'

'You don't know until you've seen it. Come on, it's best to take no chances.'

He was right, thought Cara as they went into the car park. The snow was beginning to settle and St Cuthbert's was a long drive through the hills. For Dan's sake she ought to accept the lift.

* * *

'I don't think there's any doubt about it,' said Jake, holding Dan's plump little arm and examining it carefully. 'Look at the depression on the lower arm. It's a greenstick fracture—he'll need an X-ray and plaster.'

Mrs Monkton, the nursery school attendant, looked anxiously at the two doctors. 'Oh, dear, and we're so careful here—there's mats all round the slide. What exactly is a greenstick fracture?'

'It usually occurs in children when sudden force causes only the outer side of the bent bone to break. It normally heals quickly and successfully.' Jake looked down at Dan's pallid complexion. 'He's in shock, so the quicker we get him to the hospital the better.'

Cara cuddled the little boy to her. 'Don't worry, my lamb. You'll be better soon. Lots of boys and girls do this sort of thing.' She gave him a kiss, and turned to the anxious nursery school attendant. 'We'll take him right away—and thanks for letting us know immediately.'

'I'm so sorry, Dr Mackenzie. Do let me know what happens.'

The accident and emergency department at St Cuthbert's was like most A and E Departments in the evening. A waiting room full of a variety of disconsolate-looking people sat under the eye of an enormous wall-mounted television that kept up a background hum of football commentary. A group of youths in a corner gave loud cackles of laughter, a baby was crying.

'Does this take you back a few years?' said Jake with a wry smile as they went to Reception.

'It certainly does—reminds me how much hard

work it was!' Cara looked down the corridor, seeing staff hurrying between cubicles and porters pushing people on trolleys. 'You did feel at the centre of things, though—you never knew what was going to turn up next!'

The triage nurse obviously knew Jake. 'Don't worry,' she said. 'It looks worse than it is tonight—these are mostly waiting relatives. I think Dan will be seen very soon.' She smiled kindly at the frightened little boy. 'We'll take you through right away for an X-ray and then we'll put a light plaster on that arm which will stop it hurting.'

The staff nurse who bustled into the cubicle after Dan's X-ray was plump and motherly. She flicked a switch on the wall and a brightly coloured mobile began to turn round, flashing lights. Dan looked up at it fascinated as he sat on Cara's knee, his attention diverted.

Nurse Carter smiled. 'Isn't that great, Dan?' Gently she took his arm and, talking pleasantly to Cara and Jake, began to slip a heavy gauze tube on his arm. Dan hardly noticed.

'As you probably guessed,' she said, 'you can see by the concave ''dish'' where the break is—just a tiny crack on the radius.'

She started to wind the wet plaster bandage round the arm. 'Now, when this is done, Dan, and quite dry, you'll be able to have people write lots of messages on it—perhaps draw pictures!'

Dan's colour had begun to return to his chubby cheeks. He looked up at her with a bright smile. 'I can show it to my grandpa—he's in this hospital!'

'Is he really? Then he can put the first picture on, can't he?'

* * *

Gordon Mackenzie looked up with delighted surprise when Cara, Dan and Jake came into his room.

'Why, what's happened to you, young man? Been in the wars?'

'I've been plastered!' said Dan proudly. 'Now you've got to write on it, Grandpa.'

'The first one to do so—I am honoured!'

The elderly man wrote down the side of the plaster, 'To my wonderful grandson from his loving Grandpa.' Cara felt a lump in her throat as she looked at the words. She had done the right thing to come back to Ballranoch. Her son had found a grandfather to dote on him, and her father had found a new reason to live again.

She flicked a look at the notice on his bed, NIL BY MOUTH, and frowned. 'You're not having your bypass tomorrow are you?'

Gordon nodded and smiled drily. 'That's why it's specially good to see you—bucked me up no end! Apparently they think I'm stable enough to take it, and I'll be delighted to get it out of the way.'

Cara put her hand on her father's arm. 'I'll be back in the morning to see how things are. Will you be able to manage, Jake?' she asked, looking up at his tall figure leaning against the wall.

'Of course—no problem.' He looked fondly at his older colleague. 'You take it easy now. The practice is in very good hands.' He paused for a second. 'Like father, like daughter. Cara's a great person to work with!'

'I'm glad things are working out between you. You and I seemed to get on very well, didn't we?' He looked out of the window. 'You'd better get that little boy back to his bed. The snow looks pretty fierce and your car's not suitable if you hit any drifts.'

'That's why Jake's brought us—his car's more powerful and it's got chains. We'll be fine.'

He nodded, looked speculatively at Jake and Cara, and a fleeting smiled crossed his face. 'That's kind of you, Jake. Now, off you go and let me get some shut-eye!'

The car was travelling through a white world. The snow had stopped and now every branch and building was covered with a thick layer of icing-sugar white. It looked like something from a Christmas card. Dan had fallen asleep in the back of the car, firmly strapped in and his arm supported by an arm rest. Cara leant back in her seat and closed her eyes. Just as she'd got one worry out of the way with Dan, another popped up to take its place. She wondered how her father would stand up to the rigours of a triple bipass, how she'd get to the hospital tomorrow, and if Annie would mind looking after Dan.

She flicked a look at Jake. She was grateful to him for the lift, but that was another worry. Whatever they'd assured her father, working with this man wasn't going to be easy and she saw months of edginess between them.

Jake's deep voice suddenly cut into her thoughts. 'Anything the matter? You seem very tense.'

'Not really…just Dan and my father, I suppose.'

He glanced at her quickly. 'You know there's nothing to worry about with Dan, and Gordon will be a new man after his operation. There's something more to it than that—tell me.'

She was silent, twisting her hands together. Then

she gave an inward shrug. What did it matter if he thought she was prying? She had to find out more about this man—after all, they had to work together. She flicked a looked at him under her lashes.

'You're a hard man to fathom, Jake.' She smiled.

He raised an eyebrow. 'What do you mean by that?'

'Not many men would have disregarded last night altogether—you must have taken a dislike to me!'

He looked straight ahead, manoeuvring the twisting roads carefully. 'Don't be ridiculous,' he said roughly.

'Perhaps you were told never to kiss colleagues, then?' Her tone was bantering.

His hands tightened on the steering-wheel, his knuckles white. 'I don't like to endanger working relationships,' he muttered. 'And perhaps I'm frightened…'

'Frightened? For heaven's sake. What of?'

The light from the porch lit his face and he turned to look at Cara. Suddenly she noticed that his eyes were not just a deep blue—they had green flecks in them as well. He touched her cheek with his hand, and a slight smile lit up his saturnine face for a second.

'Frightened you'll find out about my dark secrets!' he said lightly.

A cynical expression flitted across Cara's face. He was frightened all right—frightened of getting entangled with a single mother and what it would do to his career! She lifted Dan gently out of the back seat and turned to look at Jake.

'We certainly wouldn't want to do that,' she said drily. 'Thanks for the lift. I'll speak to you tomorrow.'

Jake looked in the rear-view mirror at Cara as he drove away, hugging her little boy against her in the cold whilst she opened the door. There was some truth in what he'd said. He wanted to keep his private life just that—private! What was the point of telling her about his disabled sister? Cara would think it ridiculous that Ursula would stand in the way of a relationship. But, of course, there was much more to it than that. Ursula had seen him through medical school, scraped together enough money to keep them going, and it was indirectly because of him that she'd ended up being mugged and left with her terrible injuries. There was no way he would desert her and send her into a home, and there was no way he could expect a wife to cope with his sister's jealousy and possessiveness.

He put the car into a low gear and started the climb up to the old cottage where he lived with Ursula. She'd be in bed now, but he knew there'd be an inquisition in the morning as to why he'd been so late. He smiled wryly to himself. He'd better keep quiet about the looks of his new colleague, the way her lashes fanned onto her cheekbones, the scattering of freckles on her upturned nose, the delicious little hollow in her neck that he longed to kiss whenever he saw her. Ursula would only see Cara as a rival for his affections, someone who might take him away from her—and her control.

CHAPTER SIX

CARA glanced at her watch in irritation. Why was it that when she wanted just three things at the supermarket there was only one checkout and ten people in front of her with groaning trolleys? She'd come in early on a Saturday morning, having dropped Dan off to play with a friend from the nursery. She was going skiing with Karen, but they had to get to the slopes soon for the days became dark very early at this time of year. When her father came home from hospital the following week there would be precious little time for recreation and she intended to make the most of it.

She really needed to get out onto the slopes for a breath of fresh air and exercise, Cara reflected. The past few weeks hadn't been all that easy—ever since the night when they'd brought Dan back from the hospital there'd been a tension between Jake and herself. He'd been perfectly courteous, but remote. It was as if he was deliberately keeping his distance, trying not to get drawn into any discussion that didn't involve work. Sometimes she felt stifled by the atmosphere and longed to tell him to lighten up, even ask him outright if he'd prefer that she didn't work with him at all!

And yet she had a feeling that despite himself Jake Donahue wasn't too averse to her. Why else come into her room to discuss something trivial to do with work at the end of the day when he could have left a note? Why else come round to see Dan so much at the week-

ends? Even though Dan's arm had now healed and
there was no excuse to ask how it was, often Jake
would turn up with a new game at a Saturday lunchtime. Dan looked forward greatly to these visits, and
was always talking about Jake. Sometimes Cara found
their growing intimacy unsettling.

She reached the head of the queue and fumbled in
her purse to pay. She was darned if she'd allow all
this to bother her—even though Jake's image did seem
to creep into her mind far too often, and when he did
come near her heart beat a nervous tattoo against her
ribs. If he wanted to keep his distance, so would she,
however uncomfortable it was!

The slopes were teeming with skiers and snow-
boarders, many of whom had come from Edinburgh
or Glasgow for the weekend. Karen's husband, Ian
Taylor, was operating the drag lift, and grinned as they
showed him their passes.

'Hope you've got your long johns on,' he said, 'It's
bitterly cold up there!'

Karen was just ahead of Cara and teamed up with
another woman beside her. Cara glanced up at the person she was to go up with and swallowed very hard.
Deep blue eyes in a strong face looked down at her,
and a firm mouth lifted in a slight smile.

'Seems like we're paired off together—I'll take the
far side,' said Jake.

Cara stared at him, completely taken aback. She was
about to spend ten minutes in the closest physical
proximity with the man who'd been keeping her at
arm's length for weeks!

'Why are you here?' she asked baldly. 'I didn't
know you skied.'

'When I can. I'm on duty here this afternoon. I'm part of the mountain rescue team that's always around, and we help to police the slopes amongst other things. We try and stop people going down the slopes like maniacs and crashing into others if we can. I told you before, we're short of people and I got an urgent call today to help make up numbers as two of the team are off ill. As it's a Saturday, I can manage that.'

She took her place by his side and slid a nervous glance towards him. He looked pretty good in his ski outfit—tough and athletic, goggles pushed back over a thick woollen band round his head. He had a rucksack on his back and a strip across his back that said, MOUNTAIN RANGER.

She swallowed as their lift got nearer. 'Actually, I'm not an expert on these drag lifts. I seem to fall off them rather a lot—and take my partner with me!'

He looked down at her with a light-hearted chuckle as if the astringent air had banished his usual restraint. 'Let's see how we go on, then—I dare you to knock me flying!'

Ian slipped the wood behind them attached to the spring-loaded wire that pulled them up the slope, and in no time at all she was pressed firmly against Jake's thighs. Immediately her legs slid over to his side and she stiffened, fighting against the support it gave.

'Oops! I'm not very good at this!' she admitted, giving a little shriek. 'I can't seem to keep control!'

'Are you trying to push me off?' Jake murmured, bracing himself against her weight as they were pulled upwards. 'You're certainly stronger than I thought!'

She felt his muscular legs pressing against hers, forcing her back into her own tracks. 'Sorry,' she gasped. 'I'm not doing it on purpose! Aagh!'

A sudden bump in the tracks forced her ski over his and for a horrible moment she imagined them both falling off and rolling down the slope together in a tangle of arms, legs and skis!

'You don't get rid of me that easily...' Jake put one arm round her and bodily lifted her from his skis and back into her space. 'Now,' he murmured, 'keep your legs straight and relax. With any luck we'll reach the top soon before you knock everyone over!'

As the lift came to an end there was a dip on the pathway. Skiers were supposed to let go of the wooden support and glide towards the exit, leaving the lift to carry on again down the slope. In a sudden panic, Cara let go far too early and after wobbling precariously fell over right into Jake.

'Hell!' murmured Jake's voice in her ear. 'Is that how you always leave the lift?'

With a vice-like grip he pulled her upright and she slid in an unsteady way to the side with her legs wide apart and his arms still guiding her. Then gradually, despite his support, she began to topple over. Clutching despairingly at him, she fell in an undignified heap to the ground, pulling him with her.

He pulled himself up quickly and then hauled Cara up with him, using both arms round her to steady her. He looked very gravely at her for second, then suddenly threw back his head and gave an uninhibited bellow of laughter. It was as if the weeks of tension had melted away with that one embarrassing fall of hers!

'You're like an uncoordinated octopus,' he spluttered. 'Everyone in range of you is in danger!'

Cara looked at him with uncertainty. Was he really being humorous, relaxed with her?

'I'm glad you're amused,' she said primly, then added more pointedly, 'At least I've found something to make you laugh!'

Jake gave a wry smile and nodded. 'Perhaps I have been rather too…serious over the past few weeks. I've been thinking that maybe it's time to lighten up. If we're colleagues, then we ought to be friends!'

His arms were still round her, strong, all-enveloping, and as he looked down at her it was as if that spark they'd had on the island had re-ignited. She saw the laughter in his eyes fade and something very like tenderness take its place. Cara forgot the other people on the slope flying down all around her. The laughter and shrieks of the crowd faded and in that moment there was just Jake and herself, pressed together, and the lightning of incredible attraction flashing through her. His body was muscular and hard— and she felt intoxicated and yet terrified to be held so firmly against him.

Surely she wasn't imagining that Jake felt it, too. If he really wanted to keep her at arm's length he'd drop his grasp on her, wouldn't he? There was something in that steady blue gaze and tight grip of his that seemed to signal he wasn't all that ill-disposed towards her after all.

He smiled wryly down at her. 'I'd forgotten how exciting skiing could be,' he said in a slightly husky voice.

What was it that had built up this powder keg of pent-up energy between them? Had the clear champagne-like air intoxicated them, or was it the sudden freedom of the slopes?

'You…you seem very relaxed,' murmured Cara. 'I

was beginning to think you couldn't laugh with me again…'

For answer, he hugged her closer to him, and she gave a sharp intake of breath. She had to get away from Jake before she made a fool of herself—like kiss him full on the lips or bury her head into his warm neck!

'Race you to the bottom,' she yelled, escaping from his grasp and plunging down the slope as fast as she could with legs as wobbly as jelly and her heart clattering against her ribs.

It became a magical, fun day—the sun sparkling overhead in a cerulean sky, the air crisp and invigorating. Jake seemed a different man, carefree, relaxed and enjoying himself, as if the vigorous exercise had cast out some of his reserve. Karen and Cara did sedate runs whilst he flew up and down, occasionally waving to them and sometimes trying to persuade some of the young hotheads not to snowboard directly in the line of the skiers.

If skiing is all it needs to relax a tense, moody person, reflected Cara as she watched Jake zoom down ahead of her, executing perfect turns on the slope, she'd prescribe it to all her patients!

At the bottom of the run was a large hut which served hot drinks and snacks. The women decided to rest after about an hour and Ian joined them, rubbing his hands.

'It's looking a bit black over there,' he said, jerking his head down the valley. 'We'll be stopping the lift soon and I guess Jake will be doing a final run to make sure everyone's off the slope. We want to finish well before it gets dark.'

Cara sipped her hot chocolate appreciatively. It had been a marvellous time, but she needed to get back to Dan. Just as she started to gather her things Jake came into the hut, his large frame seeming almost too big for the room. He came over to Ian, pulling off his goggles.

'Hate to tell you Ian, we've just had a call from a hill-walker that two people have been spotted under Ballranoch Tor, one with a possible leg fracture. Both are probably hypothermic. I've got a rough fix on their position, but the man's mobile keeps cutting out. We'll need to get going whilst it's still light.'

'How many rescuers have we got?' asked Ian.

Jake pulled a wry face. 'Just three of us. I've got my medical stuff with me and I'll contact the air ambulance when I get a better idea where they are. With any luck we'll be able to get there before the cloud comes down.'

Cara stood up. 'Let me come with you,' she suggested. 'At least I've some medical expertise—and you said you needed help.'

Jake glanced at her, frowning. 'No, I couldn't do that. You haven't done any training yet in mountain rescue.'

'You tell me as we go, then! Is it difficult terrain?'

'Not really—we'll traverse all the way on our skis. The tor is actually only round the bulk of the hill here. I'd take a guess that they've been incredibly stupid and started skiing off piste where there's a lot of rocky outcrops just waiting to trip someone up. I don't think they'll be far away.'

'Well, I may not be much good on drag lifts, but I can handle the skiing OK,' remarked Cara. 'All I'm concerned about is picking up Dan from his friend's house.'

'I can do that—no problem,' said Karen quickly. 'Annie will be waiting at the house, won't she? She'll be delighted to have him to herself for a while!'

Cara shot her a grateful glance. There was no short-age of help round here when it was needed.

'Would you? That's really kind. I'd like to see what happens in a mountain rescue—besides trying to help. It would be good to get the experience.'

'Well, then,' said Jake, hoisting a large pack onto his shoulders, 'if you're sure, we'll set off now.' He looked at Cara assessingly. 'You look as if you're wearing plenty of thermal clothing—the temperature will plummet when the sun goes behind the hill. Ian and Max, his twin brother, make up the rest of our depleted team. We'll set off together and as we get nearer we'll spread out a bit in a "critical search pattern", as it's called, keeping an eye open for the victims or any of their dropped possessions.'

'Right.' Cara nodded. A frisson of excited interest went through her as she wondered what they would come across when they reached the stricken people. It felt good to be involved in something that would hopefully lead to a happy outcome.

Ian introduced her to his brother Max—to Cara's eyes they seemed identical! Then they started to glide over the snow in single file, the sun still bright above their heads.

'Watch out for rocks,' warned Ian. 'The snow is very uneven here with all the drifting that occurs when it's windy.'

It didn't take long to circle the bulge of the hill, and immediately Cara felt the temperature drop as the shadow of the mountain fell in their path. It looked menacing and forbidding, and completely different from the gaiety of the ski-slopes they'd left behind.

'Spread out now,' instructed Jake. 'If you see anything, yell!'

A few minutes later, Max shouted out and waved to them. 'To the right! Twenty-five degrees east!'

Cara followed the three men as they descended to the lee of a large rock where two figures were huddled together, one of them raising an arm. They could hear a feeble cry of 'Help' as they traversed over to them. Cara squinted through her goggles at the ground in front of her. It wasn't easy. They were going quite quickly and every so often a bare patch of rock showed blackly through the snow. She gritted her teeth—there was no way she could let the team down and injure herself!

'Will you look at what they're wearing?' muttered Jake as they reached the young couple lying frightened and white-faced against the rock 'Those T-shirts wouldn't keep a fly warm!'

The girl had been crying. 'Thank God you've come!' she whimpered. 'My boyfriend's hurt his leg badly, and my arm's really painful!'

'What are your names?' asked Cara.

'I'm Sally and my boyfriend's Bob. We crashed over some stones just under the surface of the snow...'

The three men were swiftly opening their rucksacks and the twins each took out a bulky object like a sleeping bag. 'Buffalo jackets,' explained Ian briefly as they swathed the patients in them. 'Got to get their body temperatures up.'

Cara nodded, noticing the confused and glazed expression of the lad. She knew the dangers of hypothermia, how it could quickly lead to disorientation and sleepiness—lethal combinations on a freezing hillside when one was lost and injured.

'If we can just get their body temperatures up by even three degrees in the next half-hour, it could make a difference between being alert or in a coma,' said Jake, pulling a structure out of his bag which sprang up into a kind of tent. 'This shelter's windproof and if we all get in, our bodies should raise the air temperature.'

He handed Cara a small instrument. 'Take a printout of their blood-oxygen saturation levels and BP with this oximeter—could be useful information when we get them to hospital.'

Cara placed the peg of the instrument onto Bob's finger, noting the readout of his pulse and other functions.

'His BP's low—eighty over fifty,' she murmured. 'He looks in shock to me—pallid, sweating.'

Jake bent down and slit the boy's ski-pants with a knife and very gently peeled back the material. He looked at the leg carefully and pursed his lips.

'No wonder he's in shock—this looks like a compound fracture,' he said quietly to the other three. 'The skin's punctured across the tibia, and that's probably a piece of bone protruding through the wound.'

Sally's colour had begun to return. She looked much more alert, but very anxious. 'What's happened to him—what's he done to his leg?' she said in a high, frightened voice.

'He's fractured his leg, but the good news is we can give him immediate first aid to try and stop infection getting into his wound and splint the limb prior to getting him away from here.' Jake's voice was kind and he patted Sally comfortingly on her shoulder as she started to cry. 'Let's just have a look at your arm first,' he said gently. 'See how serious that is.'

Sally drew it gingerly out of the buffalo jacket and looked in alarm at a huge black bruise that covered her lower arm. She gave a sharp intake of breath. 'Oh, heavens, look at that. What have I done to it?'

'It looks very painful,' said Cara, 'but it should heal well over the next week. We'll put a sling on it to keep it still. I don't think you've broken anything from the way you're able to move it, but it'll have to be X-rayed in hospital.'

Sally's face looked stricken. 'It's the first time we've been skiing properly. We were trying to get away from the crowds. It seemed nice and empty here, but it got so cold...' Her voice trailed away miserably.

Ian and Max delved into their packs and brought out sterile dressings and a square to make a sling.

'Och, well, next time you'll know to stay on the piste where there's always help at hand—and perhaps wear something a little more robust! The mountain's no place to take a gamble with the weather.' Ian's smiling eyes took the sting out of his words as he started to put on the sling, and Sally gave a watery grin.

'I don't know if I'll be doing this again,' she whispered.

Jake was laying out a collapsible splint, snapping the joints into place. He looked up at Cara.

'Before we strap this splint on I think we'll give him 10 mils intravenous morphine to keep his pain under control.'

'Yep. I'll cover the wound, try and keep it as clean as possible.'

Cara looked round at the little team, impressed at the quiet and efficient manner way everyone worked together and the comforting way the twins were talking to Sally, reassuring her and keeping her calm.

Bob had begun to come round slightly and he gave a deep groan. 'What's happened to my leg?' he said in a slurred voice. 'It's so painful…'

'You should feel more comfortable soon—we've given you something for the pain,' said Cara soothingly. 'I'm afraid you've broken your leg, so we'll have to support it with a splint before we move you.' She turned to Jake and dropped her voice. 'I hope we can get him out of here soon—his pulse is a bit thready. Where does the helicopter come from?'

'I have rung them,' said Jake. 'It's not an air ambulance this time as there isn't one available. It's an RAF helicopter so it won't have the equipment on board I would like—still, it's a darned sight better than lugging Bob and Sally three miles down the hill. As it is, they can land a few hundred yards away on a plateau by this ridge. We three men can just about stretcher Bob that far and, perhaps with your help, Sally can walk it.'

It was fascinating to see the stretcher being put together—all that equipment in three bags, thought Cara wonderingly. Then they heard the clatter of the helicopter above them, and Ian went out to wave to them and signal them that the patients were ready to move.

'Cara, you and Sally go ahead—path-find for us, so that if you see any dangerous holes or ravines you can let us know. We'll take this slowly.'

It took nearly fifteen minutes for the small convoy to get to the helicopter, by which time two of the crew had met them and helped the stretcher party to carry

Bob. Cara puffed out her cheeks in relief. It hadn't been easy walking through the tough terrain, supporting Sally.

'I shall go with Bob and Sally in the chopper to the hospital,' explained Jake. 'Cara, you go back with Ian and Max to the lift. Thank God it's still light. By the way, you did a good job.' His eyes twinkled at her. 'You'll be getting used to helicopters soon!'

'As long as I don't have to fly them,' Cara remarked, pulling off the thick woollen hat she was wearing.

He smiled down at her, his eyes watching the wind sweep her hair into a wild halo. 'Don't forget that I still owe you a meal you promised you'd have with me,' he said softly. 'We'll arrange that next week— no getting out of it! What do you think?'

Cara's cheeks dimpled. The day seemed to be getting better and better! 'I'd love to—as long as there isn't a helicopter mixed up in the evening!'

'That's a promise, then!' He started to make his way towards the machine, then stopped and turned round. 'Damn! I'd quite forgotten. Could you do something for me, Cara? I've got a present for my sister in my car—it's her birthday and I bought it this morning on the way here. I don't want her to feel neglected! If I give you the keys, could you get it from the front seat and put the keys back under the mat of the driver's seat?'

'Sure. Shall I take it to her?'

'If you would. I don't know how long I'll be at St Cuth's, but our cottage is only about ten minutes up the hill from Ballranoch.' He scribbled down directions on an envelope and gave them to Cara.

'Tell her I'll be back as soon as I can. Oh, one other

thing. My sister—she's rather disabled. It could take her a little while to answer the door, and also…' Then his voice trailed off as if he'd changed his mind about saying anything else.

'Yes?' asked Cara.

'Nothing. It doesn't matter. Thanks for doing that.' He turned and strode off.

Cara felt a wave of happiness go over her—he seemed to have forgotten his hubris over the night they'd spent on the island and his consequent cooling off. Suddenly it seemed they could be good friends after all.

The cottage was a lovely whitewashed building with a wonderful view across the valley. Ivy had grown over the door, giving it a soft, unmanicured look that was rather attractive. Cara knocked on the door—there didn't seem to be a bell—and after a while a sharp voice called out.

'Who is it?'

'It's Jake's colleague from work, Cara Mackenzie. I'm just delivering a parcel he asked me to bring to his sister. He'll be delayed—he had to deal with an accident on the hillside. Two skiers were hurt and he's gone with them to hospital.'

Cara heard the woman click her tongue impatiently, then a bolt was drawn back and the door opened. A woman in a wheelchair looked up at Cara. She had deep blue eyes just like Jake's, but as the long black hair which shielded one side of her face fell back, it was as if a beautiful painting had been cruelly defaced. A terrible raised white scar ran right across the woman's cheek and down to her neck. Where the scar met her eye socket, the muscle had become twisted, the skin puckered and drawn. Ursula Donahue had clearly been very beautiful, but the terrible trauma her face had suffered had made a travesty of that loveliness.

Cara swallowed, masking her shock at the sight of the injury. She wondered what terrible accident had caused it, and a thousand thoughts raced through her mind. She remembered her father saying that he believed Jake's sister was very reclusive—now she understood why. She was puzzled, though. Surely these days plastic surgery could have restored some of the cheek muscle, removed some of the livid scar? As a doctor, she was surprised Jake hadn't suggested that to her.

She pushed these thoughts to the back of her mind and held out the parcel. 'You must be Ursula.' She smiled. 'Jake was afraid he might be back very late— he didn't want you to think he'd forgotten your birthday.'

'You'd better come in,' Ursula said, propelling herself backwards and wheeling round to lead the way to a cosy room at the back of the house. 'What time will he be back? He didn't say he'd be on duty this weekend!'

Jake's sister had rather a terse, charmless manner, reflected Cara.

'Apparently some of the team are off sick—I think he's doing emergency cover for them,' she explained.

'Well, that's typical, I suppose! Thinks of everyone else but his nearest and dearest—and today of all days! Anyway, thanks for letting me know and bringing the present. I guess he must have bought it this morning!'

She stared at Cara silently for a moment, her eyes sweeping over her tall figure and face, rosy from the day's exercise. 'So you're Gordon Mackenzie's daughter, are you?' she said at last. 'How long are you going to be helping Jake, then?'

Cara smiled inwardly. Her direct line of questioning wasn't unlike her brother's! 'I don't know really. I hope my father will retire now and enjoy a bit of leisure.'

Ursula wheeled her way to a cupboard. 'So you could be working for him for some time?'

'Possibly.' Cara's reply was guarded—she didn't want to commit herself to anything yet.

Ursula smiled brilliantly at Cara, the scar making her mouth twist. 'Since you're here, why don't you have a drink with me? After all, it is my birthday. I'd like to celebrate it with someone!'

'Well, just a quick one… I've got to get back to my little boy.'

'Of course. Here, have a little red wine I've been keeping for a special occasion.' Ursula turned her wheelchair to face Cara. 'I heard you had a little boy. You and he have come back to live with your father—is that right?'

'Yes, I look after him on my own.' Cara's voice was rather defensive. There was no secret about the fact that Dan's father wasn't around, but she hated that feeling that somehow she'd failed. Toby had left her, she hadn't been good enough for him.

'I see… It must be difficult, being a single mum.' Ursula took a sip of wine and said casually, 'Tell me, how do you find working with my brother?'

'Oh, fine… He's a great doctor, a most reliable colleague.' No need to tell Ursula about the tense atmosphere there'd been between them for the last few weeks, especially now that things were easier between them.

Ursula smiled and twirled the glass in her hand, looking at the red liquid as it caught the light. 'He's worked hard to get where he is. It's not been easy, of course, but he has the ability and the perseverance to go a long way—if he's single-minded enough.' She looked steadily at Cara. 'I suppose that's why he's never sustained any kind of a relationship. Plenty of girls have been after him, of course, but they've all ended up with broken hearts! He can't afford to jettison everything he's worked for to be held back by a family!'

She laughed as if to soften her words. 'I think he's the kind of man who finds complete fulfilment in his work. It wouldn't surprise me if he eventually wanted to get higher up the ladder, perhaps become the medical officer for the local health authority.'

Cara nodded slowly. 'You could be right. He…he seems very dedicated to his work.'

Was there a hidden agenda in Ursula's words? Cara wondered. Was she trying to tell her something, prevent her from being hurt? It sounded as if Jake had been fending women off quite a lot. And it was as she'd suspected—he was an ambitious man who wanted no hangers-on. A woman with a child in tow who fell for him would be a millstone round his neck up the slope of advancement.

Ursula's words echoed in Cara's ears all the way home. It was an irony that on the day she felt Jake had put his doubts about their friendship behind him his sister should tell her the truth. The warning was clear—stay away from Jake or have your heart broken! She knew she couldn't bear to be hurt again. The pain of Toby's betrayal still seared through her, the shock of finding out the truth so brutally stamped for ever in her mind's eye. Whatever attraction she felt for Jake she would have to suppress, even though today he had suddenly seemed so…friendly.

'Hands off, Cara!' she said sadly as she parked the car in the drive. 'Dr Jake Donahue isn't up for grabs!'

CHAPTER SEVEN

'EXCUSE me, could I come past, please?'

Cara pushed her way through the long line of people waiting in Reception. It seemed unusually full and chaotic, even for a Monday morning.

'Ah, Dr Cara. Am I glad to see you!' Sheena Burnett, the practice nurse, looked up in a beleaguered way through the glass partition. 'Karen's not turned up. It's most unlike her. I've tried to ring her at her house, but there's no reply. And to top it all, the computer's crashed! Karen's the only one who understands it!'

'Wonderful! So we don't know who we've got or the order they're coming in?' Cara came through to the office and grinned at Sheena's pink, harassed face. 'My horoscope said I'd have a challenging day—it was right!'

She looked at the tottering pile of mail on the desk and the blank screen of the computer. 'Somewhere in the system are about seventy blood and biopsy results that need checking,' she said ruefully. 'I can't see us finishing early.'

At least, she reflected gloomily, she'd be too busy to think about Jake. It was a paradox that since learning from his sister that he wasn't interested in romance, she couldn't help dreaming about the man, even wondering what it would be like to be loved by him! That was why she'd kept out of his way for the past week, hoping that out of sight would be out of mind!

'This is bedlam,' snarled Sheena, grabbing the phone and answering its persistent ring.

Cara flicked a glance at the sea of faces through in Reception. 'You don't think Karen's had an accident, do you? What about Ian? Perhaps we could get him on his mobile—I think the number's somewhere here. Where's Jake?'

'Emergency call in the village. I'll try and get hold of Ian.'

While Sheena grappled with the demands of the office, Cara went back to Reception and held up her hand. 'Quiet, everyone,' she said loudly. 'We've got a bit of a glitch with the computers this morning, so we don't know the order of our patients. Would the person booked in for eight-thirty come to my room now? Dr Donahue shouldn't be long.'

Two people immediately stood up and stared obstinately at each other, one obviously being Jake's patient, the other Cara's. 'I'm the eight-thirty appointment,' they said in unison.

'Then I'll see you in alphabetical order.' Cara smiled at them sweetly.

Her first patient was an old gentleman with a badly inflamed finger. 'I was pruning my roses,' he explained. 'I always do them in early spring—and a thorn gave me a very deep jab. Now it's throbbing away and very sore. I told my wife it would be all right, but she insisted I come here.'

'She was quite right, Mr Dunne,' said Cara. 'It looks painful and very red and hot. If you'd left it untreated it could spread quickly to other areas. Cellulitis—infection of the tissues—must be treated quickly. Can you remember if you've had an antitetanus injection in the last five years? I can't bring that information up on the computer at the moment, I'm afraid.'

'Aye, I had one not so long ago.'

'That's good. No need to repeat that, then. However, I want you to take one of these tablets four times a day—that's very important—and finish the course.' She handed him a prescription.

The elderly man frowned. 'One tablet four times a day?' he repeated slowly. Then he smiled. 'I'm a stupid old fool—I was trying to work out how you could take the same tablet four times!'

Cara laughed. 'That will teach me to be clearer! Come back if it hasn't improved in three days. I'd like you to keep the hand elevated. If Sheena can put a sling round it, that would be a help for you. If you wait, she'll do it for you when she has time.'

She followed him to the door and caught sight of Jake. He smiled when he saw her patient.

'Ah, Peter! Glad I've seen you. I was about to reply to the invitation you sent me for the exhibition. I look forward to coming, thank you very much. And I hope to buy one of your paintings this time.'

'Aye, it'll be a good evening. I've done quite a bit of work over the past year. Make sure you come early. And it's not just my work, you know—we're trying to get other local artists to contribute.'

The old man stumped off to speak to Sheena, and Jake turned to Cara. 'Peter Dunne's a local artist—he does wonderful landscapes of the countryside round here,' he explained. 'He's having an exhibition next week.' He looked quizzically down at Cara. 'I've been meaning to ask if you'd like to come with me and perhaps we can have that meal I mentioned? You seem to have been very elusive this week—it's been hard to find you.'

Cara flushed slightly, her heart thumping at his proximity. 'I don't want to commit myself at the moment,' she said quickly. 'My father's coming home this week, and I can't make any long-term plans.'

An expression of disappointment crossed Jake's face. 'Fair enough,' he said abruptly. 'I think you would have enjoyed his work though. Perhaps another time.'

'Perhaps. The immediate future looks pretty busy for me, though,' Cara said firmly.

He frowned slightly. 'You seemed happy with the idea of a meal out the other day,' he remarked, watching her face closely. 'Why the quick change?'

'I told you, Dad will need a lot of care. I can't leave him on his own.'

'I'm not asking you to leave him for days on end—just a couple of hours one evening. Annie will be there, won't she?'

Cara felt a sense of panic. Jake might well be asking her out for a friendly evening's chat so why get so worked up? Because he's too darned attractive and sexy for a platonic relationship, whispered a little voice inside her.

'I don't know. I'll see what happens,' she said lamely. She flicked a glance behind him at the full waiting room. 'Perhaps we'd better get on—don't want a riot on our hands!'

The morning was chaotic as Sheena had her own work to do, taking blood pressures and changing some dressings. Cara and Jake helped her out where they could, taking phone calls and arranging ambulance pick-ups for the elderly patients who couldn't make

their appointments without a lift. Then halfway
through the morning the phone went for the fifth time
in ten minutes. Cara took the call.

'Ian Taylor here. I got a text message from Sheena
asking what had happened to Karen. I went back to
the house and I've just found her stumbling around,
talking a load of gibberish! She seems completely out
of it! Could someone get here quickly? It looks really
bad!'

There was panic in his voice. 'Don't worry, Ian,'
soothed Cara. 'I'll be there right away. You're only
just down the road.'

She went into the office where Sheena and Jake
were having a restorative cup of coffee after the hectic
morning.

'The good news is that Karen's been located,' she
announced. 'The bad news is that Ian's found her in
a most peculiar state—it all sounds very odd. I might
need some diagnostic assistance—it sounds as if it
could be anything from a stroke to drugs!'

Jake and Sheena looked at each other in astonishment. Karen was young, healthy and sensible—the last
person one would associate with either a stroke or an
overdose.

'I've got to make a call further down the same
road,' said Jake. 'I'll pop in with you on my way, if
you think two heads would be better than one.'

'You'd better get off right now, both of you,' sighed
Sheena. 'I'll hold the fort. Just get Karen better again
soon, or we'll all collapse!'

Cara and Jake bent over the restless Karen. Jake prised
open her eyes and frowned. 'Pupils are quite dilated,'
he murmured. 'More than you'd expect.'

'She seemed out of her mind,' said Ian worriedly. 'Kept going on about some pop star of all people and how she was longing to see him! But her sentences were all disjointed, and when I put her on the bed she tried to get up but couldn't.'

'Is she on any medication that you know of? It looks almost as if she's accidentally overdosed!'

'She'd never do anything like that!' cried Ian indignantly.

Cara patted his arm. 'I know she wouldn't. I'm just saying that it's as if she's had something inadvertently, or perhaps had an accidental dose of some sort of substance that's had this affect on her.'

'Her pulse is very fast,' said Jake. 'It's extraordinary. How was she when you got up this morning?'

'Absolutely fine,' said Ian. 'I went out first to take young Kirsty to school, and left Karen to have her usual bacon and eggs.'

'Perhaps the bacon was off…some sort of food poisoning?' suggested Cara. 'Let's look and see if there's any left in the fridge.'

'I'll watch her—you go and see if you can find evidence there,' said Jake, covering the woman up with a rug

Cara peered into the fridge and saw an opened packet of bacon which she took out and looked at carefully. 'It's well within the sell-by date,' she remarked. 'Smells quite fresh, too.'

She put it back on the shelf and then paused for a second before closing the fridge door. 'Hang on,' she said slowly. 'What's this on the shelf above?'

She took out a small container lying on its side above the bacon and inspected the label. 'I have a feeling that this is the culprit,' she said with a wry smile at Ian. She handed him the packet of bacon. 'And I think you'd better throw this away—it's got a lot to answer for as well!'

Ian looked at her, mystified, as he followed her upstairs to the bedroom. 'What on earth's up?' he asked.

Cara held up the container in front of Jake and Ian. 'Your little girl, Kirsty—she has a lazy eye, right?' she asked. 'I guess she's been prescribed these atropine drops, which have to be stored in a fridge.'

Ian nodded. 'That's right, but I don't see how...'

Jake gave a short laugh. 'I think I know what you're going to say. The atropine container has fallen over and some of the contents have dripped onto the bacon and contaminated it! Am I right?' He looked at Cara with raised brows. 'Well done, Miss Marple!'

Ian scratched his head. 'What do we do now?'

'If the hospital was nearer we might take her there for observation,' said Cara. 'I don't know if Jake agrees with me, but I think in the circumstances if you could stay with her and ring us immediately if her condition changes for the worse, the effects of the atropine should wear off in a few hours. She already looks a little more relaxed.'

Jake felt Karen's pulse again. 'It's slowing down a little now. We'll get Sheena to pop in and out during the day anyway.' He smiled at Ian's dumbfounded face. 'What Karen's had is a dose of deadly nightshade! That's where atropine comes from—and it's a very useful drug, but not taken orally!'

'You learn something new every day,' Jake remarked as they drove back to the surgery. 'Now you know that it's possible to get spaced out on eyedrops!'

He parked the car at the side of the house which was reserved for the surgery and looked enquiringly at Cara. 'Had any more thoughts about coming to the art exhibition? I really think you'd enjoy it, and I know Peter's done some lovely paintings of this house overlooking the loch.'

Was she being churlish to refuse an invitation like this? Cara reflected that she was probably making more of it than he'd intended—after all, it was only a few hours, not a lifetime commitment! Jake had been so kind to Dan and a tower of strength to her father— why be unsociable just because she felt her knees go weak whenever she saw the man? She'd just have to learn to control her emotions! He was a colleague and she needed to keep on friendly terms with him.

'Thank you,' she said primly. 'I'd like to come and see the paintings very much!'

'It's a week tomorrow, so your father should be settled at home by then. We'll go to the exhibition first and have a meal afterwards. I'll pick you up at about seven o'clock.'

As soon as the alarm went off Cara knew in the pit of her stomach that the day was going to be a long one. A week had gone by since Jake had asked her to go out with him, and it had gathered speed relentlessly. It was a paradox that the next twelve hours would crawl by!

She dragged herself out of bed, half dreading, half looking forward to the evening, one minute telling herself that it would merely be an interesting outing to see some paintings, another minute wondering crazily if she and Jake might end up in each other's arms again. Cara pushed that thought firmly to the back of her mind as she washed. Ursula had told her candidly that Jake had other priorities than getting involved in relationships, and she would ignore that advice at her peril. The evening would be polite and friendly, full stop!

There was a sudden bang and her bedroom door was pushed open violently. A small body hurled itself into her arms.

'Don't want to go to nursery school today,' announced Dan firmly.

'Why ever not, Dan?'

''Cos Grandpa's home now, and he says he'll miss me. I could look after him very well—he said I could be his little nurse!' Dan looked up Cara with his hands on his hips, and his bottom lip stuck out obstinately. 'He said so!'

Cara laughed—it was impossible to be down for long when her son was around. 'Grandpa's got to rest a lot—he can do that while you're at nursery school. When you come back he'll have more energy and you can tell him everything that's been happening—he'd love to hear that!'

She bent down and picked Dan up, hugging his plump little body to hers. 'Come on, let's have breakfast in Grandpa's room for a change, and then we'll leave him to have a sleep!'

Gordon was propped up in bed, reading the newspaper. His face lit up joyously when Cara and Dan came into his room.

'Ah, it's my little helper!' he said jovially. 'Buchan's been telling me that you took him for a lovely walk yesterday with Annie by the loch.'

'Did he tell you that himself?' said Dan seriously.

'He was a very naughty dog—he went in the loch and shook himself all over Annie when he came out!'

Gordon laughed, his eyes meeting Cara's in amusement over the child's head, and she was struck by how well her father looked after his bypass operation. Gone were the purple lips and sunken eyes—his face had a healthy pink complexion and he looked bright and focussed. He was a different man to the frail person she'd seen on the night of her return. Hopefully he had put all the heartache that Angela had caused behind him, and it was wonderful to see the loving relationship that existed between him and his little grandson.

Was it only a few weeks ago that she'd watched her father collapsing before her on the dance floor on the night of hogmanay? She shuddered. If it hadn't been for Jake's prompt action her father might not be here now. There would have been no time to build bridges between them.

She bent down and kissed him on his cheek. 'Feeling better now, aren't you?' she said softly.

Her father nodded and said gruffly, with a quick loving look at her, 'You'll never know how much. Only one thing I miss, and that's my pipe!'

'Don't you dare!' scolded Cara. 'I'll have you struck off if you light up!'

Gordon grinned. 'You're a tyrant,' he said affectionately. 'By the way, Jake tells me you're going to Peter Dunne's art exhibition tonight. I'd love to have gone—he's a great artist. Look out for anything he's done in this area, would you?'

Cara's heart rattled against her ribs for a moment as she was reminded of the evening's activity. Jake and herself together for at least three hours! She was beginning to wish she'd never agreed to go!

'Come on, poppet,' she said firmly to Dan. 'Time you and me were off for a day's work.'

'Bring me back a painting you've done at nursery school, Dan,' said Gordon. 'I'll put it up on the wall in front of me.'

Dan nodded and spread out his arms. 'Yes, I'll bring you back a *'normous* one—this big!'

Cara looked without much enthusiasm at the row of clothes in front of her. In the last few months shopping had not been a priority—just keeping her sanity looking after a little boy, a job and coping with the betrayal of a lover had meant there'd been little time or inclination to devote to herself.

She pulled out a crêpe navy trouser suit and held it up against herself, looking critically in the mirror. Teamed with a pink silk blouse she felt it would be suitable for the occasion. She gave a wan smile as she remembered that she'd been with Toby the last time she'd worn it, and he'd told her she looked good in it. But, then, he had fastidious taste when it came to clothes.

Pushing that unwelcome recollection to the back of her mind, Cara coiled her springy hair into a chignon at the back of her head, holding it in place with a comb, and flicked a little blusher on her cheeks, trying to disguise the day's tiredness.

'That will have to do,' she said to herself in the mirror. 'Now, let's get it over with!'

Jake was waiting for her downstairs, sitting in a chair with Dan on his knee whilst he read the little boy a book. A reading lamp shone down on them, spotlighting their two heads together in a pool of light, and Jake's face was turned towards the little boy's with a tender, amused look. Cara caught her breath. This was how it should be always for Dan, she thought wistfully—someone like Jake to take time with him, to be a father figure for him. A lump came to her throat. No chance of it being Jake, not with his career ambitions.

'Right, I'm ready.' She smiled.

Jake looked up and his gaze darkened as it lingered over her for a minute. He set Dan down on the floor and went over to her.

'I like the hairstyle,' he murmured. 'You look… very beautiful…'

Dan giggled. 'Mummy, Jake says you're very beautiful!'

Cara turned to him quickly, glad of the chance to look away from Jake for a moment and hide her blushing cheeks. 'Now, shoo! Off you go to bed. Annie will read you another story if you're a good boy.'

'Your carriage awaits,' said Jake, grinning at her as if he sensed her discomfort.

The gallery in Ballranoch had been converted from an old barn and had high ceilings, with huge windows which allowed in a lot of light during the day. Now it was bright with electric light, and crowded with people enjoying a glass of wine and canapés as they looked at the paintings.

Cara began to feel more relaxed as she sipped some wine and felt the buzz of the social atmosphere. It was good to do something different to the usual daily round, be a part of the little community.

Jake watched her animated face as she talked to old

friends. She looked as if she was enjoying herself. He noted how the trouser suit skimmed her tall, slim figure, and the chignon of hair emphasised that beautiful long neck. She look sexy, lovely and very desirable! His mouth tightened. Had he been a fool to have asked her out? Every time he saw her he was convinced that if he'd been free she would have been his choice. He took a long sip of wine and sighed as he followed Cara with his eyes. There could be no future for them together—not with Ursula's dependence on him.

Moodily he twirled the now empty glass in his hand as he remembered his sister's conversation with him after she'd met Cara.

'Quite a glamour puss,' she'd remarked coldly, watching Jake's reaction to that remark. 'She's obviously in need of a husband—wouldn't surprise me if she hadn't got her beady little eyes on you, dear brother. You want to be careful, or you'll be trapped with a child to look after!'

Jake smiled sadly to himself. He knew what made Ursula say sour things like that—it was terror. She was so scared of being left on her own, lonely and unloved. He put his glass down and bunched his hands in his pockets, gazing unseeingly at a painting in front of him. Of course he would never leave his sister alone— he loved and admired her very much. She had sacrificed too much for him, he reflected, losing her beauty and her social confidence as a result. Now it was his turn to make sacrifices.

Cara tapped him on his arm. 'What do you think of this?' she asked, leading him to a large painting.

It was of her father's house set against the magnificent background of mountain and loch, obviously painted in late summer when the heather stained the hills purple.

'Don't you think my father would love it?' she said.

He looked down at her sparkling eyes and enthusiastic face and smiled. 'I'm sure he would. It's a wonderful painting.'

'Then I'm going to get it!' she declared. She looked at Jake with a slightly devil-may-care expression. 'It may be I've had too much wine, but I'm in a buying mood, feeling a bit reckless. I'm going to make the most of it!'

Jake grinned. 'Then perhaps we'd better go and eat before you buy the rest of the gallery!'

It was raining softly as they left the gallery. Jake put up his umbrella and slipped his arm through Cara's, bringing her under its protection.

'Must be getting near spring,' he remarked. 'At least the snow's turned to rain.' He steered her up a small side street. 'The restaurant's up here. I think it's quite good, although there's not much in Ballranoch to compare it to.'

Cara laughed. Suddenly it was good to be out, and much to her surprise she was enjoying the evening, but she didn't allow Jake to draw her any closer as the rain increased in intensity.

There weren't many people about. In front of them an elderly woman was taking her dog out for its nightly walk, and there was a youth coming towards them, his shoulders hunched, a baseball cap on his head.

Cara didn't really notice what happened next, it was so quick and unexpected. The youth suddenly veered off towards the old lady, then snatched a bag from her shoulder and with a burst of speed disappeared back up the street.

There was a distressed cry from the woman as she staggered back against the wall at the impact, and a roar of fury from Jake. Cara watched, open-mouthed, as he took off in front of her, disappearing in the direction the youth had gone.

Cara ran up to the old lady, standing in a dazed way by the roadside.

'What happened?' the woman said tremulously. 'That lad banged into me, didn't he? He's taken my bag!'

Cara put her arms round the trembling woman. 'Don't worry, you're all right. I'm here. Lean on me and we'll go and sit down for a minute.'

The victim allowed herself to be led into the restaurant, where the staff leapt round to sit her down and bring her a warm drink. Her little dog followed her and sat down beside her, the two of them looking forlorn and bedraggled.

'The young hooligan!' said Cara, filled with sympathy for the frail old lady. She held the woman's hand. 'How do you feel? Did he hurt you at all?'

'No... I...I just feel a bit shocked, it was so sudden.' The victim put up a trembling hand to her head as if confused by what had happened. Then with a sudden burst of spirit she said bravely, 'I'd teach that rascal a lesson if I met him again—I'd set the dog on him!'

'Good for you, love, don't let it get to you!'

Seeing that the old lady was being well cared for by the restaurant staff, Cara went out to see if she could see Jake. Coming down the road were two figures. One was Jake and the other was a sullen youth he was propelling in front of him.

'We'll wait here,' Jake said grimly. 'The police will be coming soon, and I hope they throw the book at this young oaf.'

'I never hurt her,' whined the boy.

Jake twisted the boy's face up to his, his blazing eyes an inch from the boy's. 'Didn't hurt her? Do you think that poor old lady's going to forget about this? It will stay with her for the rest of her life, you little toad. You need thrashing, picking on a vulnerable person like that.'

Cara looked at Jake's expression. There was something of a white-hot fury about him, as if this particular crime might send him over the edge. She felt it wouldn't take much for Jake to lose it completely and take a swipe at the youth. Then he'd be had up for assault!

She touched his arm lightly to try to bring him back to a more rational mode. 'I'm glad you've caught him, Jake,' she said quietly. 'Let the police deal with him – I think they're coming now.'

Jake almost threw the boy at the sergeant who came up. 'You take him—I might do him a mischief!' he growled. 'I suppose you want us to come and give statements, do you?'

The policeman nodded. 'If you would, sir. We'll try not to keep you long.'

Jake looked at Cara wryly. 'This was meant to be a relaxing evening. Don't worry, we'll finish it later!'

The youth was driven away by the police, and Jake went into the restaurant with the old lady's bag which he handed to her. He sat down by the old lady and took her hand. 'Why,' he said gently, 'it's Winifred

Batley. I managed to rescue your bag, Winnie. I hope nothing's lost from it.'

An impish smile suddenly broke out on the old lady's face. 'There wasn't much in it—just my laxative tablets, and he'd be welcome to those!'

Jake smiled, but his tone was grim. 'I can think of other substances I'd rather give him. Anyway, Winnie, there's a police car waiting to take you back home and the police want to hear from you what happened. Dr Mackenzie and I will go to the station and give our statements, and I'll be calling on you in the morning to see if you're all right. Would you like me to ring your son and tell him what's happened?'

Winifred looked at him gratefully. 'Aye, doctor, I'd appreciate that. He'll come over to be with me, I know.'

Jake turned to the owner of the restaurant. 'Keep that meal on hold for us, Carlo—the evening's not over yet!'

CHAPTER EIGHT

CARA looked curiously across at Jake as they sat in the cosy half-light of the restaurant. His expression was brooding, lips compressed as he examined the menu. She was surprised at how near the edge he'd come to losing it completely with the mugger. It had been as if a different person had emerged from the self-contained man she'd thought she knew.

He caught her looking at him and smiled, as if trying to shake off his gloom. 'Never let it be said that I've given you a dull evening!' he commented wryly. 'I think we deserve an injection of wine—something smooth that slips down easily.'

Cara nodded. 'That would be nice. I feel I've almost been mugged myself. It happened so quickly! I thought a little place like Ballranoch would be safe enough from crime.'

'Unfortunately not. These hooligans prey on the vulnerable even in a beautiful village like this. I don't like to tell you what I'd do to them if I had my way.'

She glanced at him with perception. 'The attack on Mrs Batley really affected you, didn't it?' she said gently. 'At least she wasn't physically harmed. It could have been worse…'

Jake blue eyes darkened angrily. 'As I said to that young thug, poor old Winifred will have many sleepless nights because of him. You know yourself that it takes a long time to get over a mental trauma, and I venture to think that Winifred's peaceful frame of mind has been shattered. She's old, and she may never feel safe walking alone again.'

'That's true. Having her son to talk to will help, though,' suggested Cara. But Jake was right about mental trauma, she reflected sadly. There were some things she could never erase from her mind.

'What really gets me,' said Jake savagely as if he hadn't heard Cara's remarks, 'is the fact that that lout will forget all about his actions in a week or two—it won't make a jot of difference to him. I know that it's changed Winifred's life for ever.'

Suddenly his eyes seemed to focus back on Cara, and he gave a shamefaced smile. 'Sorry. I'm afraid I do have a thing about street violence—I must stop going on about it. After all, we're supposed to be having a pleasant evening. I'll try and forget about it. Now, let's choose something to eat—I hope you're hungry.'

'Starving,' she admitted. 'It seems ages since lunchtime. I could eat a horse!'

Jake grinned. 'Let's hope it doesn't come to that! How about some fresh bass in a white wine sauce with prawns? Light but filling. And then I suggest the most wonderful hot pecan pie with thick cream.'

Cara shrugged off the suit jacket and leant back against her chair. 'Sounds very sinful, but I'm willing to put aside my principles. I'll start the diet tomorrow.'

Jake's eyes swept over her, noting how the pink silk blouse enhanced the glow of her skin in the muted lighting, and how her breasts curved provocatively against the constraints of the material.

'The last thing you need to do is diet,' he observed gravely. 'There are too many stick insects about, and too much emphasis on eating as little as possible!'

There was something about the intimate way he looked at her that made Cara's heart suddenly start to flutter, and she took a quick sip of wine. She mustn't misinterpret his actions, she thought firmly. He was merely making a social observation.

Jake ordered their meal, then turned back her. 'By the way, I never thanked you for delivering my sister's birthday present last week. I did try to but, as I said, you were difficult to catch!'

'It's been a busy week,' murmured Cara. She looked at him speculatively. 'Does your sister work?'

'She works from home. She's an artist and does landscapes like Peter Dunne, but in a very different style.'

'What a pity she didn't go to the exhibition tonight, then. Wouldn't she have been interested? Surely artists like to get together and discuss each other's work?'

Jake poured some more wine into Cara's glass before replying. 'Ursula doesn't go out very much… she's a very private person,' he said at last. 'She used to be very gregarious but, as you can see, she has bad facial scarring. It…it's changed her personality, I'm afraid.'

Cara frowned. 'I wondered…' she said falteringly. 'I know it's none of my business, but did she ever think of some sort of facial reconstruction? The maxillofacial plastic surgeon at St Cuth's is supposed to be marvellous. Of course, I don't know how she did it, and perhaps it's too difficult a job.'

Jake shrugged his shoulders. 'I have tried to persuade her—believe me. But she's absolutely adamant that she won't go through any more pain. I think the trauma of what happened to her has turned her into…well, into a different person. As I said before, it only takes a moment to change someone's life for ever.' His expression was incredibly sad and for a few seconds there was silence between them.

Cara put her knife and fork down and regarded him sympathetically for a moment. 'How did it happen?' she said softly. 'Was it a car accident?'

Jake shook his head. 'No, nothing like that, although if it had been an accident she might have got over it better. I'm afraid to say it was deliberate.'

'What do you mean—deliberate?' whispered Cara, her eyes wide with horror.

His face was grim. 'I can remember as if it were yesterday,' he said in a low voice. 'Ursula was attacked in the street by a gang of drunks, looking for money to feed their drug habit. I was walking some way ahead of her, and it was me they were trying to get. They knew I was a doctor and supposed my bag might contain something they could use. Ursula realised they were going after me and tried to prevent them.'

'How did she do that?'

'She was like a wild thing, biting, kicking them, but she never stood a chance. They battered and stabbed her, but still she wouldn't give in. Then they ran off when I came back to intervene. I never even received a scratch but poor Ursula was in hospital for many weeks.'

Cara looked at Jake's face. It was drawn with misery, the pain of the event still raw in his mind, and she realised why he'd lost some of his objectivity when Winifred had been mugged. She put a hand across the table and placed her hand on his.

'It wasn't your fault. You don't blame yourself surely?'

He smiled sadly at her. 'I'm afraid I do to some extent. You see, I'd already told her to hurry up and keep up with me as we were late for a meeting. I'd even said that she shouldn't have bothered coming if she couldn't get there on time!' He paused for a moment as if gathering his thoughts. 'You see, Cara, if I'd been less impatient I'd have been by her side when it happened and able to fend off her attackers. Yes, ultimately I believe it's my fault that Ursula received her appalling injuries.'

Cara shook her head. 'You're being far too hard on yourself—you must know that. Has Ursula ever said she blamed you?'

'Never. All the same, I owe her so much—not just for that night, but for my life generally.'

'In what way?'

He grinned, his countenance lightening somewhat. 'I wasn't born with a silver spoon in my mouth, I'm afraid. I come from a long line of idlers who preferred drink to work, and after my mother died my father didn't care what I did as long as I didn't cost him money. It was Ursula who was ambitious for me—struggled to find the money to see me through medical school.'

'You have a lot to thank her for, then.' Cara toyed with her knife and fork for a second. 'It's good that you and she live together now, isn't it? She must love that.'

'We're very close. It suits us both.'

As Cara sipped the coffee they'd ordered, she reflected that, of course, it would suit a bachelor to have a sister in tow. He had a ready-made excuse not to get involved with anyone. He had to look after his sister, and she was there to cook and wash for him—it was

a perfect shield to protect him from any predatory fe-
males!

She flicked a look at him from under her lashes.
Whatever his sister had done for him, Jake was to be
admired for his support of Ursula. He had a strong
sense of loyalty, and underneath that tough exterior
there was an affectionate and loving nature.

Perhaps it was because she felt sorry for Jake, perhaps because she wanted in some small way to thank
him for the lovely meal, but on the way home Cara
found herself saying rather diffidently, 'How about
coming in for a quick nightcap? My father keeps a
good malt whisky.'

She looked at Jake's profile next to her in the car.
She was beginning to understand why he had a touch
of the loner about him. He wanted to do as well as he
could in his career to make up for his sister's sacrifice,
and that needed drive and perseverence. Ursula had
told her that he'd had to eschew a romantic life to
pursue his ambitions, and single-minded people often
seemed rather aloof.

Cara's path through medical school had been very
easy compared to Jake's. Her parents had been encouraging and there'd been enough money to see her
through. It had just been the latter part of her life that
had fallen apart, she thought sadly.

The embers of the fire were still burning in the huge
fireplace in the drawing room, and there was an air of
cosiness and warmth about the place. The dark red
velvet curtains were drawn, and the only lights on
were the reading lamps by the easy chairs. Cara tossed
another log on the fire and it sprang to life, sparks
flying up the chimney and making their two shadows
dance on the wall opposite.

Suddenly shy, she glanced at him rather timorously, wondering why she'd gone against her better instincts and asked him back. It seemed just slightly too intimate—just the two of them together in the sheltered atmosphere of the cosy room.

'Do you like water with your whisky?' she asked.

He stood well away from her as if he, too, was embarrassed by the situation they were in. 'No, I like to taste the real thing.'

Cara passed him a glass and then stood by the fire. There was silence between them for a few seconds, then they both spoke together.

'When are you going to show your father his picture?'

'I can't wait to show Dad the picture!'

They looked at each other and laughed, the tense atmosphere between them easing. Jake moved towards her and took a mouthful of whisky.

'Good stuff, this,' he said, holding up the glass to the light then looking round the room. 'This is such an elegant room. Where do you think you could put the painting?'

'If Dad doesn't want it in his bedroom, we could always put it above the fireplace.'

Jake looked at the spot she indicated and nodded. 'Yes, I'm surprised there isn't anything there now…it seems the perfect place.'

'There was a picture there once—a portrait,' said Cara sadly. 'It was of my mother, but dear Angela made sure it was removed. I suppose it was hard to expect a young bride to keep a huge likeness of her husband's first wife in the house—but nevertheless it hurt me to see it gone. She was a very beautiful woman.'

Jake gazed at Cara gravely. 'Then you take after your mother.' He leant against the mantelpiece and said slowly, 'I hope you don't mind me asking—but how did your father come to meet Angela?'

Cara bit her lip—it still shook her that her father could have married so soon after her mother had died. 'He met her at a medical conference—she was the manageress of the hotel where it was held. I couldn't believe it really—my parents had been married for twenty-five years and adored each other, but Mum had only been dead for six months when my father re-married. I think he was trying to fill the terrible gap in his life, but he couldn't have chosen a more unsuitable person.'

'So he didn't know her before?'

'No…he was taken in by her looks and honeyed words, I'm afraid. Angela was only concerned with one person—herself! She saw money, a title and a vulnerable man who thought she loved him for himself…' Cara gave an unsteady laugh. 'They say there's no fool like an old fool, don't they?'

'I take it he was besotted with her, then. And from what you said before, you were forced out?'

Cara looked at the leaping flames of the fire, twisting her hands together. 'I'm afraid my relationship with Dad started to crack from then on. The truth is, he was so frightened he'd lose Angela that he'd do anything to accommodate her wishes. Angela wanted me out of the house but Dad objected to me going with Toby. He saw him for what he was—a pretentious rat.'

'So what happened next?' prompted Jake gently.

'We had a terrible row and he said he didn't care what I did as long as I didn't annoy Angela!'

Cara's words hung starkly in the air, their very simplicity highlighting the terrible shock she'd felt at the time. It was surprising how the retelling of the story moved her, and to her embarrassment two large tears rolled down her cheeks. She hunched her shoulders and hugged her arms round herself as if trying to suppress her emotion.

In an instant Jake was by her side, his arm round her shoulders, his forehead creased with concern. 'Cara, sweetheart…please, don't get upset. I wouldn't have mentioned it for the world if I'd thought it would hurt you. Forgive me for prying…'

Cara brushed her tears away angrily. What was the point of getting upset over something that was done and dusted now?

'Don't be silly—it's not your fault,' she said with a catch in her voice. 'I'm a fool for allowing myself to cry over a horrible woman like that. As a matter of fact,' she said with a faint smile, looking up at him with eyes still moist with tears, 'it's good to talk about it. Toby didn't like maudlin introspection.'

'He doesn't sound a very sympathetic character.'

'No,' said Cara shortly.

Jake hooked a finger under her chin and lifted her face to his. 'So…no more tears?'

He held her glance for a moment, and Cara began to breathe a little faster. He was so close she could see the dark flecks in those blue eyes, the late night stubble on his chin, feel his breath on her cheek. Any closer and they would be touching, breast to breast. His arm was still round her shoulders and suddenly it seemed natural to Jake to draw her closer, pull her head down onto his chest, rocking her against him like one would with an upset child.

She heard the steady thump of his heart and gulped. He was like a rock, his muscular body holding hers comfortingly, soothing her as his hand stroked her back. He was merely being kind, she told herself sternly, it was nothing to do with attraction or need. He was just trying to calm her because she was upset—wasn't he?

She looked up at him before pulling gently away. 'You're very kind…' she started to say.

'Cara…' His voice was rough, his eyes dark with longing. 'Cara, don't move away. I…I want to kiss you so very much, comfort you.'

Then he bent his head down, and suddenly his mouth was on hers, setting her lips on fire, teasing them apart and melting them in a long and passionate kiss. For a second she made a feeble effort to resist.

'Jake, we mustn't allow ourselves to get carried away,' she mumbled.

Then her limbs dissolved into jelly as his lips moved down to the sweet little hollow in her neck and from there to the swell of her cleavage, covering the soft skin there with the lightest of butterfly kisses.

How could she stop herself responding when trails of electric desire flickered through her body, delicious sensations turned her insides to liquid? She wound her arms round his neck, pulling him closer, straining against him and abandoning herself to a sea of passion that washed over her, helping her to forget the anguish of her father's remarriage and Toby's betrayal. She was powerless to do what she knew she should—pull right away from the man, force him to stop!

'God, but you're beautiful, Cara—every inch of you,' he whispered, his hands fumbling for the buttons on her blouse. He pulled the garment gently away from her, unhooking her bra so that her breasts spilled out of it, full and soft.

The rug was soft, the flickering fire still warm as he pulled her down beside him. His face looked down at hers, strong in the half-light, and his hands were magical, touching her body so that it screamed with arousal. Then his body straddled hers, hard and demanding, and she melted against him, unable and not wanting to stop what he was doing.

Cara closed her eyes and turned her face towards his, waiting for the kiss she expected, then opened them again when nothing happened. Jake was staring down at her, a tormented expression on his face. With a low groan he rolled over to one side and lay on his back with his eyes fixed on the ceiling.

A bleak feeling of disappointment filtered through her. 'Is…is something the matter?' she whispered anxiously. 'Are you all right?'

He sat up and shook his head, his voice harsh. 'I'm sorry, I shouldn't have done that—not started making love to you. I was just overcome by how beautiful you are, but I should never have led you on…. It's unfair of me.'

Cara sat up and stared at him, a feeling of acute embarrassment mixed with hurt filling her. She felt confused—one minute she was in his arms and he was fiery in his passion, the next minute he had drawn away from her and was telling her he shouldn't have led her on. Bitterly she reflected that she should have known from Ursula's warning that Jake went so far with relationships and no further. In a way it was her fault for being so easily seduced, allowing something like this to happen. Then a cold fury gradually overtook her and her eyes blazed across at him.

'What do you mean, you shouldn't have done it? How could you lead me on, pretending that you were trying to comfort me, taking advantage of my situation? You…you're nothing but a *louse*.'

Jake sat down on a sofa and put his head in his hands. 'I know,' he muttered. 'It was despicable, I should never have touched you.'

Cara buttoned up her blouse and moved over to the fireplace, away from him, sickened at how easily she had gone along with him.

'Too true,' she snapped. 'You've made a fool of me—but I should have known.'

'The trouble is, Cara, I couldn't help myself,' Jake said in a low voice.

She looked down at him scornfully. 'Don't give me that—I'm just one in a long line, aren't I? One of the many women whom you've seduced and then cast aside because you're too focussed on your damn career.'

His face darkened and he stood up, facing her with a frown. 'It's not like that at all. What do you mean? Perhaps it's not a good idea for colleagues to be too close, but it's nothing to do with my career—what gave you that idea?'

'I heard the truth from your sister. I should have listened to her, shouldn't I? She warned me that you'd had plenty of girls flinging themselves at you to no avail. Well, let me tell you something, Dr Donahue, you don't need to worry that Dan and I will hold you back from the ladder of success!'

'That's simply ridiculous!' Then he looked at Cara silently. Ursula had been through too much on his account, and loyalty to his sister held him back from explanations. He didn't want to imply that Ursula would stop him having a relationship, or that he felt it was unfair to Cara to saddle her with the responsibility of his sister's life.

He put his hands on Cara's shoulders and looked into her stormy eyes. 'I'm so sorry,' he said gently. 'You can't know how much I wish things were different. The best thing is to try and keep our relationship on a strictly professional basis from now on.' His eyes swept over her lingeringly, a touch of sadness in their depths, and he said in a low voice, 'Don't think too badly of me, Cara. We have to try and work together.'

'How can we work together?' she burst out. 'The whole situation is ridiculous! OK, perhaps being too close to a colleague might not work for you—but one thing I know for sure, that being one of your cast-offs isn't going to work for me either! In the circumstances, over the next few weeks I shall be keeping my eyes open for another job—somewhere a little more relaxing, where my colleagues can be trusted!'

They stared at each other for a second, then he turned and left the room abruptly. Cara watched him leave, and tears started pouring down her face. How could he have done this to her—allowed her to experience the heady heights of passion and then snatch it all away? She dabbed her eyes and gazed unseeingly into the crackling fire. It was all too horribly familiar, this scenario, she thought bitterly. They said experience was a great teacher, but she had learned nothing from the past, and now she had been humiliated yet again.

CHAPTER NINE

JAKE DONAHUE stared gloomily in front of him. He hadn't looked once at the article in the medical journal he'd picked up ten minutes ago. The truth was that he couldn't bring himself to be interested in 'Inner City Hygiene—Methods for Managing Waste Effectively.' All he could think of was Cara and how he'd humiliated her—the last person on this earth he wanted to hurt!

He'd been a fool to think that his good intentions of comforting her when she'd become upset would stop at that—a soothing cuddle. Somehow his longing to make love to her had completely taken over, and for a second he'd allowed himself the fantasy that they could be together. As if, he thought wryly, a future together would ever work—a young mother having to cope with a possessive and jealous sister to whom he owed everything.

He scowled and threw the journal down. He'd been selfish, and now he had to pay the price. Cara barely talked to him and when she did it was polite but terse and very, very chilly. And to make matters worse, he knew she was looking for another job!

He jumped when the buzzer rang stridently in his ear, glad of something to divert his thoughts.

'Yes? What is it?' he said abruptly.

'There's a visiting patient here in a lot of pain. Could you see him before lunch, Jake?'

There was a slightly reproachful air about Karen's

voice, which made Jake wince. He knew he'd been short and irritable with everyone for a few weeks now—ever since the catastrophe with Cara. He would have to start sounding more mellow, or even dear Karen, now back hale and hearty in Reception, would barely talk to him!

'Better send him in then,' Jake said in a gentler tone.

Jake looked up as a pleasant-looking man with short blond hair came through the door, and his expression changed to one of surprised pleasure.

He strode round his desk and shook hands with him. 'Why, Chris! Chris Renshaw! Haven't seen you in ages—not since we were housemen together! I thought you lived down South. This isn't your usual patch, is it?'

Chris Renshaw shook his head, and said in rather an indistinct voice, 'I was staying with my aunt in the village for a night or two to do some fishing. I meant to contact you, but she'd arranged a dinner party round me so I hadn't the time—and now I'm on my way home for a wedding.'

'So this isn't a social visit, then?'

'Not exactly,' said Chris, smiling rather sheepishly. 'I need your professional opinion. I'm afraid, as a thoracic surgeon, my knowledge seems to be mostly about the chest cavity! I know it's your lunch-hour, but your receptionist took pity on me.'

'Of course! Whatever you're here for, it's great to see you! How can I help?'

'I'm finding it a bit difficult to give my cheeky smile or eat at the moment,' explained Chris. 'My jaw's stiffened up overnight and I can't open my mouth more than about a centimetre.' He added wryly,

'People are always telling me I'll get lockjaw from talking too much—and now I think they're right!'

Jake pursed his lips sympathetically. 'I should think you're in a lot of pain.' He felt the man's jaw, trying to wiggle it gently and see what movement he had. 'You probably realise your jaw's become partly dislocated. The muscles are in spasm, preventing the jawbone from relocating.'

'That's what it feels like. It's darned uncomfortable—is it my TMJ?'

'That's right—temperomandibular joint dysfuction! A short course of Valium should relax the muscles, and anti-inflammatory painkillers will reduce the swelling.'

'At least I might be able to eat and sleep properly then,' mumbled Chris.

'You ought to see a dentist as soon as possible—perhaps a gum shield at night could prevent the problem recurring.' Jake grinned at Chris as he printed out a prescription for him. 'We haven't seen enough of each other since we worked together—and since those days I believe you've acquired a wife and several children, right?'

'That's right! Three little ones. Best thing I ever did was to marry Jenny. Never regretted it, even though my golf handicap's gone up!' Chris raised his brows enquiringly at Jake. 'What about you? Don't tell me you're still fancy-free.'

Jake grinned ruefully. 'Afraid I'm still a dedicated old bachelor—and likely to remain so.'

'I seem to remember you were the man everyone thought would fall off the shelf first!'

Jake's laugh was rather forced. 'I don't think I've

got your touch when it comes to women. Perhaps I've too many excuses not to take the plunge!'

Chris looked at him sharply, as if sensing he'd touched a nerve, and said casually, 'How's your sister? I remember how badly injured she was by those brutes when we were housemen together.'

'I wish she'd get out more, but I'm afraid she's been really antisocial since then. Absolutely refused to have facial reconstruction, although I did my best to persuade her.'

'She was a very brave girl—give her my regards.' Chris stood up, folding his prescription and putting it in his pocket. He held his hand out to Jake who shook it warmly. 'Thanks a lot, Jake. I'm very grateful to you.' He paused for a second, then said lightly, 'Next time I see you I expect to see you hitched. *Tempus fugit*, you know—remember, no one can wind back the clock!' He turned at the door and gave a salute with his hand. 'I'll be in touch—so long!'

For a few seconds after Chris had left, Jake stared at the screen in front of him. Too right that time was flying by, he thought. He'd been a GP here for five years and in that time Chris had got married and had children—moved on, in fact. In another five years would he, Jake, still be here, a bachelor living with his sister? He sprang up from his desk in irritation and went into the corridor, standing for a moment outside Cara's door. Why didn't he just march in and tell her that he loved and adored her, and to hell with his worries about his sister? Chris was absolutely right!

He lifted his hand to knock on the door, then let it fall again. What was the point of trying to build bridges when Cara thought nothing of him now?

The door opened abruptly and Cara came out, replacing her initial startled expression at seeing him with a cool stare.

'Excuse me,' she said, sweeping past him and going into the office behind Reception. 'Karen, could you tell that rep I'll see him for lunch in a few minutes? And don't forget, I'm off this afternoon, thank goodness. I could do with a rest!'

'Doing anything nice?' said Karen.

'Taking Dan to the beach—he's got a kite and is longing to try it out!'

'Some rest!' Karen smiled. 'Mind you don't get blown out to sea!'

Suddenly Cara sat down on one of the chairs and hugged her arms round her stomach for a minute, biting her lips.

Karen looked at her in consternation. 'Got a problem?' she asked.

'No, no,' said Cara, shaking her head and grimacing slightly. 'Just a painful period, that's all. I seem to suffer that way recently. Not to worry, I'll just take a painkiller and get a really good lunch out of this rep!'

Cara lifted her head towards the sea and breathed in the sharp scent. The air felt fresh and invigorating, just what she needed after the past few weeks. A renewed surge of energy seemed to flow through her and she vowed to try and take more exercise now the better weather was coming—it might help these painful periods.

'Off you go, Dan. Take your kite! I'll lock the car and follow you.'

Dan scampered off, full of excitement at having his mother to himself and the prospect of playing with his new toy.

Cara's eyes swept over the wonderful backdrop of sea and mountain—another week or two and the bright gorse would soon be out, spreading like a golden carpet over the lower hills. Unconsciously she lifted her chin defiantly. Despite that darned man, Jake Donahue, she was going to be optimistic about the future!

Wryly she admitted to herself that it had been partly her fault that things had gone awry—Ursula had told her what the score was regarding Jake and women, and she'd taken no notice. And now, although Jake still came too often into her thoughts, he'd humiliated and embarrassed her and she had to forget about him. She pressed her lips together firmly and bent her head against the slight wind. It was time to look ahead and think of her little boy's future, and how she could do her best for him.

She watched Dan running ahead of her along the small parade that led down to the sand, holding his kite in front of him. How lucky she was to have such a perfect little son, so much fun and so energetic. It made up for everything that was happening in other parts of her life.

He stopped to speak to someone sitting on the path by the sand dunes, one of the many artists who were tempted to come and paint this part of the coastline— so dramatic with the mountains rising steeply away from the shore and the contrasting colours of sky and land. There was an easel in front of the woman and Dan was pointing at something on her canvas. Cara could see the woman throw back her head and laugh at something Dan had said. Cara smiled, knowing how winning Dan could be.

'Don't be a nuisance, Dan,' she called, starting to

run towards him. 'The lady doesn't want to be disturbed, I'm sure.'

Dan and the woman turned round at Cara's voice, and Cara realised with surprise that it was Ursula Donahue.

Ursula looked at Cara with a slight smile and a raised brow. 'Ah, so it's Dr Cara Mackenzie! If this is your little boy, he's not disturbing me in the least,' she said. 'Actually, it's quite nice to have someone ask me about my painting—although,' she said drily, 'he doesn't mince his words. Says my colours are funny!'

Dan looked at her earnestly. 'I *like* it, though. I think it's really very nice!' Then he frowned, and put a chubby hand to her scarred cheek. 'Have you hurt yourself? Is it sore?'

Cara held her breath. It was no good being cross with the child. He'd said it so sweetly, surely Ursula would know a boy of his age didn't mean to be offensive? She bit her lip and watched the woman with slight trepidation.

Ursula went very red for a second, staring in a peculiar way at the child. Then she took his hand very gently and held it in hers. 'Nobody's asked me that before. Adults aren't quite so upfront with their remarks—although,' she added wryly, 'I know what they're thinking. Sometimes it is a bit sore in the cold weather, but I think I've got used to it now.'

There was something different in Ursula's voice as she spoke to Dan—a softer, kinder timbre to her tone, less terse than usual. 'And your name's Dan, is it?' she enquired. 'Do you paint, Dan?'

He nodded solemnly. 'I paint pictures for my granddad. He puts them up in his bedroom—he says he's going to ask everyone to come and see them.' He smiled beguilingly at Ursula. 'You can come if you like!'

A gleam of humour shone in Ursula's eyes. 'Thank you. I'd like to see your paintings very much.'

Dismissing the subject from his mind, Dan hurled the kite up in the air and watched it drift down to the beach. Cara bent down and pulled up the zip on his jacket as the wind got up slightly.

'Why don't you unwind the string, Dan, and start running along the sand with it? I'll come and help you in a minute.'

He scampered off and Ursula watched his robust little figure doing his best to get the kite to rise from the ground.

'He…he's quite a little charmer,' she murmured, almost to herself. 'In some ways he reminds me of Jake when he was little…'

She looked up at Cara as if suddenly aware that she'd spoken out loud, and gave a slightly embarrassed laugh. 'I don't see many children these days,' she said, as if in explanation.

Cara smiled. 'I'm very lucky to have him,' she said. 'May I look at your painting?'

Cara drew in a deep breath of delight and amazement—it was powerful, almost three-dimensional in its approach, drawing the viewer into the landscape, flooding the eye with colour that reflected the scene before her.

'Ursula,' she gasped. 'That is the most wonderful painting. I…I've never seen anything like it. Your brother told me you painted but I had no idea you were so talented. Why don't you exhibit these paintings?'

Ursula gave a short laugh. 'Nobody would be interested in what I do,' she muttered. 'Anyway, I do them for myself, not for strangers to gawp at.'

'I can imagine these pictures giving tremendous pleasure to people—even those who don't know the area.' Cara looked searchingly at Ursula. Perhaps she really meant that she didn't want people gawping at *her*—that by going public as it were, she too would be on view.

Ursula shrugged. 'There are plenty of people painting in this area. What's the point of flooding the market with yet another version of the same place?'

'But these are so different, Ursula—a very individual interpretation. Have you ever let anyone but your brother see them?'

'No,' said Ursula shortly. 'I'm certainly not going to start toting them round either.' She looked at Cara with her funny little half-smile. 'Jake tells me you're looking for a new job—aren't things working out between you, then?'

How much had Jake told her? Cara bit her lip, uncertain how to reply. 'I might do locum work,' she said vaguely, 'then I could choose the hours I work and have more time for Dan.'

'I see—but you'd stay in the area?'

'At the moment I wouldn't leave my father—and anyway I love it round here. But if I can't find locum work round here I may have to move away to a larger town.' Then she sighed. 'This has always been my real home—where I'd really want to spend the rest of my life.'

She smiled to herself, hearing an irony in her own words. Perhaps it wouldn't be so easy to re-invent her life up here after all—not with Jake Donahue in the same area!

They heard a shout from the beach, and could see Dan waving at them impatiently. 'Come on, Mummy,' he yelled. 'Help me fly my kite!'

Ursula looked at Cara. 'Perhaps you'd better go—your little boy needs you.'

Cara walked off towards Dan, an idea forming in her head. She was no artist but she appreciated art, and she knew that the work she'd just seen was remarkable—and probably very marketable. There was something very lonely and almost prickly about Ursula Donahue—probably not helped by her injuries and the terrible way they'd occurred. Surely it would boost her confidence if she were to realise just how good her paintings were?

A little smile lifted Cara's lips. It would be good to do something positive for a talented, shy person like Ursula, even if her brother was a rat!

She picked up the kite and held it aloft. 'Go on, Dan,' she cried. 'Run as fast as you can along the beach and see how high we can make this kite go!'

A few days later, Cara found the time to visit Peter Dunne who lived at the far end of the village in a small cottage with a breathtaking garden in front of it. Cara guessed that in the summer it would be filled with a profusion of foxgloves, campanula, daisies and other herbaceous plants. A rose twined its way round the door—no doubt the one that had caused his poisoned finger a few weeks ago!

Cara rang the bell, wondering just what Peter's reaction would be when she asked him to help her carry out the idea she'd had when she'd met Ursula by the beach.

He let her in with a cry of welcome. 'Come for your

picture, then? I've reframed it as you asked, and I think it would look great in the drawing room of your father's house. Does he know about it yet?'

'No, it's a big secret for his birthday. I know he'll be absolutely thrilled.'

Peter held out his hand for her to see. 'Look at that! The poison's all gone, thanks to you, and I'm back to painting and gardening again.'

'I'm delighted to hear that.' Cara smiled. 'But the main reason I'm here is to ask a favour. Do you know Ursula Donahue?'

'Aye, Dr Donahue's sister? I know who you mean, but I can't say I've spoken to her much—keeps herself to herself, I believe.'

Cara leaned forward eagerly on the chair she was sitting on. 'Do you think you'd be able to help me if I said I wanted to persuade her to have an exhibition of her paintings?'

Peter nodded. 'Certainly, if I could. I once called round at their house to take a picture round to Jake and I remember seeing one of hers there—it was a remarkable painting done in a very individualistic style.'

'Exactly! I have a feeling she doesn't have a clue how talented she really is, and I think it would be wonderful for her to show her work. Give her a separate identity to being merely "the doctor's sister". Jake once told me that you liked to encourage local artists, so what do you think?'

'I'd certainly love to persuade her—but how could we go about it? She'd not like to push herself forward or put herself in the public eye.'

'Well, it could all go pear-shaped, but St Cuthbert's Hospital has a transplant unit that's second to none, and I know they're trying to raise money for vital new diagnostic equipment. Since my father's had his by-pass he's been very keen to get something off the ground to help, and I wondered if we could have an art exhibition at the hospital. If we could coax Ursula to contribute, it would be great.'

'Yes, she might feel more inclined to go public, as it were, if it was for a good cause. In fact, I think quite a few artists would be prepared to do something like that—give a proportion of their sales for the equipment.'

Cara looked pleadingly at Peter. 'Could you explain it to Jake? Perhaps he could persuade Ursula.'

'With pleasure, lass. But wouldn't it be easier for you to do that? After all, you work with the man!'

'You're the one who knows how to set these things up—I wouldn't have a clue where to start,' Cara said quickly. 'Anyway, you're the expert—he'd respect what you had to say! I have to admit, I don't want to become too involved—I'd rather Jake thought the idea came from you, if that's OK.'

Peter laughed. 'I'll do my best!'

As she drove away, Cara felt a frisson of pleasure—it might make all the difference to Ursula if she could achieve something on her own without being in the shadow of her brother. She reflected that it was probably very hard to be the sister of someone who was so ambitious—no wonder the woman was shy. It should be quite possible for the thing to be organised without her, Cara, having anything much to do with the arrangements. In that way she reflected with satisfaction, she wouldn't have to come into contact with Jake at all!

She flicked a glance at her watch—just one more visit before she went home. She had promised to see an eighty-five-year-old patient who had been seen by the community nurse that morning. Nellie Parsons was a frail old lady and Cara had become very fond of her in the past few weeks. She was an endearing and cheery lady, but there was evidence of abdominal bleeding and Cara had arranged for Nellie's younger sister to be at the house when she called.

Beattie, the sister, met her at the door, her mouth pursed disapprovingly. 'I hate letting you into a tip like this house, Doctor. I don't think Nellie's ever tidied up or thrown anything away since the war—it needs a darn good dust!'

A thin voice piped up from the next door room. 'I can hear you, Beattie—you're criticising my house-keeping, aren't you? You're a pernickity old witch! And you know Dr Mackenzie comes every week, so she's used to it!'

Cara gave an inward giggle as she picked her way over piles of magazines and cardboard boxes that covered the floor. The two sisters were always bickering, but she was sure they were devoted to each other really.

'Hello, Nellie,' she said cheerily. 'I've just come to check up on you. I believe you've been in a bit of pain, had some bowel problems—is that right?' She looked at her mock-sternly. 'Have you been having lots to drink like I told you to?'

'She has not, Doctor,' said Beattie weightily. 'She's a very stubborn woman—you told her to drink eight glasses of water a day—unless it's got whisky in it, she won't touch it!'

'Och—that's a terrible lie!' said Nellie, then both sisters started chuckling and Cara joined in.

'I don't know that I would recommend quite that much whisky,' she teased. 'Let me just take your blood pressure and then I'll take some blood for tests. We can find out a lot from that—for example, if you're anaemic or dehydrated.'

Nellie held her arm out for Cara to take her blood pressure. 'And how's your dear old dad?' she wheezed as Cara pushed back the sleeve on the old lady's arm. 'I miss seeing him so much. He knew my Bert so well—they used to go out the back and have a pipe together, you know!' She gave Cara a sweet smile. 'Not that I don't enjoy you coming, my dear, or that gorgeous Dr Donahue. I could eat him for breakfast!'

Cara unwound the cuff of the sphygmomanometer very carefully. 'Could you now?' she said lightly. 'Be careful—he's single, you know!'

Both ladies gave snorts of laughter, and Beattie said knowingly, 'Oh, there'd be a fair number of lassies willing to have him, but if he does go out with anyone he keeps it well hidden! Too much on his plate with that sister of his, I'd say!'

Cara made some notes of Nellie's blood pressure. 'So he's never had a girlfriend, then?' she said casually, still looking down at her pad as she wrote. 'I heard from somewhere that he had loads of girlfriends but never stayed the course with them.'

'If I got hold of him, he wouldn't get away so easily. He's got everything, that man—looks, lovely personality, steady as a rock!' said Nellie.

'A pity you're old enough to be his great grandmother, then,' commented her sister tartly, but with a wink at Cara.

Cara smiled a little bleakly. How come Jake Donahue kept getting such a good press from everyone who knew him? They all seemed to love him, from her own son of three to Nellie Parsons at eighty-five! Why was it only her that found him a complete rat? A tremor of loss went through her. She'd expected too much. She packed up her equipment and patted Nellie on her arm.

'The community nurse will be in tomorrow, Nellie, to see how you are. We'll have the results of the tests soon. Until then, plenty to drink, and I've given you a repeat prescription for the pain of your arthritis.'

She waved to the two old ladies at the window as she got into the car. They were lucky they had each other, even if they didn't live together. She looked at her watch. It was nearly five-thirty, time to pick Dan up. Her period pain seemed to have died away, and because she hadn't felt like eating much for lunch with the young pharmaceutical representative, she was starving now. She'd make up for it tonight with Annie's lovely rich hotpot!

CHAPTER TEN

IN NORMAL circumstances, if she hadn't had this niggling pain in her lower abdomen that seemed to be
getting more intense every minute, Cara would have
felt very sympathetic for the immaculately neat Mrs
Hunter. At the moment she was finding it hard to concentrate on the worried mother's distress.

'Just what are you saying doctor?' squeaked Mrs
Hunter. 'I just *cannot* believe that Rebecca could have
anything as…as *filthy* as impetigo! I thought she'd
caught something like chickenpox with all these little
blisters on her hairline.'

Rebecca stared at Cara in alarm behind round wire-
rimmed glasses.

'Will I have to go to hospital?' she said in a frightened voice, one hand scratching her head.

Cara forced her mind away from the annoying pain,
and smiled reassuringly. 'Not at all—I can give you
some medicine for it, so don't worry.'

'It's that school!' fumed Mrs Hunter, outrage ex-
pressed in every fibre of her body. 'There are some
very undesirable types there—probably don't ever
wash! If there's one thing I insist on with Rebecca, it
cleanliness!'

'Come here, Rebecca,' said Cara gently. 'Just let
me look at your scalp.'

Mrs Hunter threw her eyes to heaven in horror.
'Don't tell me it's there as well!'

Cara took a fine comb from her desk drawer and

drew it through Rebecca's long hair. 'Aha!' she said with satisfaction. 'I've think I've found a nit, and where there's a nit, there's been lice! I'm sure that's what's caused poor Rebecca's skin infection.'

'Nits? For heaven's sake!' Mrs Hunter looked mournfully at her daughter's thick hair. 'Will I have to cut her hair off short? That's what we did in my day. Not,' she added hastily, 'that we ever had them in my family.'

'I assure you—this is nothing to do with your daughter not being clean, and you don't need to cut her hair,' said Cara patiently. 'The fact that Rebecca has head lice is nothing to do with dirt at all. I can see for myself that her hair is gleaming. The fact is, lice are terrible pests—they don't mind if hair is clean or dirty. Probably the whole class has got them at school. Unfortunately the intense itching leads to scratching—and a bacterial infection has obviously got into the little wounds. It's really nothing to be ashamed about.'

Mrs Hunter drew herself up in chair. 'It's disgusting!' she declared roundly. 'I shall certainly keep this to myself!'

Cara sighed. The nagging pain seemed to be coming on again more intensely. She needed to get the consultation over as soon as she decently could.

'You can keep them at bay by combing through the hair when it's wet. Your next step is to go to the pharmacist and he'll give you some lotion to put on the hair— Ooh!'

She gave a little gasp as the infuriating pain seemed to increase, and Mrs Hunter looked at her sharply.

'Something the matter, doctor?'

Cara clenched her teeth. 'No…nothing, it's all right. As I said, just go to the chemist in Ballranoch….'

Mrs Hunter pursed her lips. 'There's no way I'm letting the chemist know we've got lice or impetigo in the family—he only lives next door! I'll have to go all the way to the next town to get the lotion!'

She stood up and looked resentfully at Cara as if she had somehow contributed to the lice problem. 'Thank you anyway, Doctor. Come on, Rebecca. We'd better go and get rid of this…this *infestation* as soon as possible!'

She swept out, followed by her gloomy-looking daughter, and Cara heaved a sigh of relief. Perhaps she'd have time to take some painkillers before the meeting that was going to take place in her room in a few minutes.

She sat very still for a second, willing the pain to go away, then a gut-wrenching spasm slammed into her as if she'd been kicked in the stomach and a band of perspiration broke out on her forehead. What on earth was the matter with her? Cara took a sip of water from the glass on her desk. Soon Jake, Sheena, the physiotherapist and the practice manager were coming to her room to discuss the budget for the next six months and the priorities of the practice that had to be addressed. She closed her eyes—she just couldn't face it!

She clutched her stomach again as agonising stabs of pain started to slam through her and waves of nausea gripped her stomach. Groggily she got up from her chair and then fell on the floor, curling up in agony, the room fading in and out of her sight.

'What do you think, Ursula? Won't you do it to help the heart unit? I know you keep your paintings very much to yourself, but this exhibition would do so much to raise money.'

Jake paused for a second to watch his sister's re-action to the suggestion that she should show some of her paintings. Her face was turned towards him and he felt a stab of sympathy for her, as he had on so many occasions when he saw the terrible scarring she'd suffered on his behalf.

She shook her head doubtfully. 'Oh…I don't know. I don't fancy having to mix with hordes of people. Who's organising this anyway?'

'Apparently it's Peter Dunne—you've met him be-fore. As you know, he's an artist, too, and he's work-ing very hard to set it up, but he's worried they won't have enough exhibitors.'

'Perhaps if I didn't actually have to be there,' she said hesitantly. 'I suppose if it's in such a good cause and they're really short of pictures, I don't mind.'

Jake beamed. It had been a long time since Ursula had agreed to anything as outgoing as putting her paintings on show. It might give her a new interest, choosing which pictures to exhibit and how she wanted them displayed.

'That's wonderful, sis!' he exclaimed. 'Don't worry—I'll do all the setting up if you tell me what paintings you're offering.'

'All right… I might choose that one I was doing the other day of the sea with the mountains behind.' Ursula flicked her hair back from her eyes. 'That was when I saw that Cara woman at the beach with her little boy. I must say, he's got quite a personality,' she said with a slight smile. 'He blurted things out in a very frank manner—like you when you were a little boy!'

'He's not bad, is he? His grandfather's a new man since Dan came into his life.'

His sister raised her eyebrows. 'Then he's going to be very upset when he hears that Cara's thinking she might not stay in the area for long.'

Jake put down the coffee-cup he'd been holding, and looked up sharply. 'What? You mean she's moving quite soon?'

'If she can't get the work she wants, that was the impression she gave. When her father's stronger, she said.'

Jake stood up abruptly, looking at the ground for a second, his mouth grim. Then he looked up at her with a tight smile. 'I'd better get back—I've got a practice meeting in a few minutes. I'll speak to Peter about your pictures—he'll be really pleased.'

A myriad of emotions pounded through Jake's head as he drove down the hill, knuckles white on the steering-wheel. He couldn't believe that it had come to this, that Cara would actually move away from the area! Somehow, since seeing Chris, it had made him think rather hard about his life, and how he was letting it slip away. OK, he owed his sister, but surely he deserved a little happiness, too?

Savagely, Jake wrenched the car round the sharp bend at the bottom of the hill and squealed into the surgery road. Cara thought he was playing her along, that he was too ambitious for a long-term relationship and that she and Dan would hold him back. It wasn't true, but that's what it seemed to her.

He had held back for a variety of reasons, but that wasn't one of them. He loved his job, he loved the area. His dream had been to settle there and one day have a wife and family, and after all this time Cara had come into his life. Like a fool, he'd let his sense of responsibility towards Ursula hold him back because he'd thought there was no way he could make the commitment to Cara that she deserved. And now she was thinking of moving away. He parked the car and jumped out, slamming the door angrily.

He strode into Reception and picked up the papers relating to the meeting.

'Is everyone in yet?' he asked Karen.

'Only Cara so far. She's just seen her last patient, so you might as well go in—I'll bring in some coffee for you all soon.'

Jake nodded and went straight to Cara's room, then stopped at the doorway, for a second unable to believe his own eyes.

'What the hell's going on?'

Cara lay doubled up on the floor, her hair spread wildly over her shoulders and a gasping sound coming from her throat.

'Cara, what's the matter? Where does it hurt?'

He knelt down beside her, gently brushing back her hair from her forehead and putting his hand on her pulse. 'How long have you been like this?'

'It…it's been coming on and off all morning. I can't breathe with the pain…it's like a knife,' she whispered. She turned over on her back, her forehead damp with perspiration. 'Jake, I…I think something's very wrong. It's my right lower abdomen. It's awful…'

'Don't worry, Cara, I'm here,' he said in a calm, firm voice. 'I'm taking you to St Cuth's now. Sheena can come with us, and I'll phone through to A and E and get things set up for a scan.'

She nodded feebly, her eyes closed, and Jake looked down at her pale, drawn face, her lashes a dark sweep over her cheeks, her hair a tumble of auburn on the floor. And all at once, with a terrible lurch of his heart, it was as if a dusty mirror had been cleaned and he saw things clearly for the first time. All other considerations faded away into the background. Was he going to lose her just as he realised that she was all he wanted in his life? He needed her, body and soul.

He couldn't stop himself. He bent down and kissed her damp forehead. 'It'll be all right, darling—hang on there!' he whispered huskily.

She didn't answer, just gave a faint moan.

He stabbed his finger on the intercom button on her desk, his hand shaking in a most unprofessional manner, his mind racing through all the things that could be causing Cara's illness.

'Karen!' His voice was clipped and urgent. 'Come and stay with Cara for a minute. We've got an emergency on our hands—she's got acute abdominal pain and I'm just phoning through to the hospital.'

Karen looked at Cara in shocked surprise as she rushed into the room, then knelt down beside her and held her hand. 'Oh, Cara,' she said in distress, 'You poor thing!'

Through a haze of pain Cara could hear Jake's terse voice phoning through to the hospital. 'Dr Donahue here, Ballranoch Practice—I'm bringing in my colleague, Cara Mackenzie, as an emergency. She's got acute right ileac fossa pain—could be appendicitis or an ovarian problem. Can you set things up for our arrival in about half an hour?'

Jake and Sheena were taken to the small staff kitchen in St Cuth's Casualty Department by Sheena's sister who was a nurse at the hospital. Sheena sat on a chair, sipping a cup of coffee, while Jake stalked up and down the room like a caged lion.

'She should have told us she'd been feeling off for a few days,' he fumed. 'Carrying on with that abdominal pain was silly. Any other person would have gone to the doctor! She could have a ruptured appendix, an intestinal blockage…anything!'

'Keep your hair on, Jake—she's gone for an MRI scan now and they're running blood tests, so we should know fairly soon—and she's in the best place.' Sheena patted the chair beside her. 'Now, why don't you have a cup of coffee and try and relax?'

'OK,' he muttered, and sat down on the edge of the chair, staring down at the cup of coffee she handed him.

The door opened, and a short, balding man with glasses came in. Jake sprang out of his chair, dropping his cup on the floor. 'Well, Barney? What's the verdict—what have you found?'

Barney Woolerton, the consultant on A and E gave a wry smile. 'Lovely big twisted ovarian cyst, I'm afraid. We're going to operate. Connie Brown's the gynaecologist and she's going to look at Cara first. She thinks it's a haemmorrhagic cyst—there seems to be some bleeding into it.'

'When are you taking her to Theatre?' asked Jake.

'As soon as possible. Do you know how long it is since she's eaten?'

Sheena smiled. 'I happen to know that. She came in a bit of a flurry to work this morning, said she hadn't had time for any breakfast so she had a cup of coffee in surgery at about nine o'clock.'

Barney looked at his watch. 'That's nearly six hours ago—we should be all right to give her an anaesthetic now, so I should think she'll be under the knife in no time at all.'

Jake winced. 'Don't be quite so graphic, Barney,' he snapped. 'Just get on with it!'

He followed Barney down the corridor, running an agitated hand through his hair. 'What about her obs? You won't operate unless—'

Barney turned round and patted him on the arm. 'Calm down, mate! I can tell you her obs are stable. She's slightly tachycardic but her BP's holding out fine, something like one-ten over seventy...nothing to worry about!' He looked at Sheena standing by Jake's side. 'Why don't you take him to the pub for lunch?' he suggested. 'Let us get to grips with things!'

Cara stretched gingerly. The wound in her abdomen still hurt, but the terrible searing pain had gone, and a few days after the operation she felt surprisingly well. The whole incident seemed like a hazy nightmare. She could hardly recall being taken to hospital, although she knew that Jake had lifted her out to his car, could still remember the rough feel of his jacket on her face as he'd lowered her onto the back seat. She flushed. She had rather it had been anyone other than Jake who'd seen her in such an embarrassing state, being sick, as she recalled, all over the floor of his car!

She looked out of the window of the little side ward she'd been allocated, and felt a sudden sadness come over her. Perhaps it was just post-operative blues, or too much time to think about herself, but the future seemed to have lost its promise. That sense of loss she'd felt earlier came back more vividly than ever.

She'd come back to Ballranoch with such high hopes of making it up with her father, giving Dan a better life—and then there had been the bonus of being attracted to the gorgeous Jake Donahue! More than attracted, she thought wistfully. She had to admit, she'd fallen totally in love with the man.

Only it hadn't worked out. She'd allowed herself to believe he felt something deeper than attraction for her, and she'd been wrong. There wasn't room in a two-handed practice for an uneasy relationship and when she felt better she'd have to look for pastures new. She blinked back a few tears of self-pity. There seemed to be a pattern developing in her life—going somewhere for a new start, and then it crashing down about her ears! She hunched the sheet round her shoulders as if she were cold, and felt a bitter finger of sadness touch her heart.

There was a soft knock on the door, and Cara sighed. So far the only visitors she'd seen had been Dan and Karen, and it was hard to seem welcoming at the moment to anyone else.

'Come in!' she called, trying to sound upbeat.

The door opened and Jake stood there, dwarfing the entrance, with a huge bunch of flowers in his hand. He looked down at her strangely, a kind of nervous suppressed energy about him.

'I've got to talk to you,' he said tersely.

Cara's eyes opened wide. 'Jake! I hope you got my message from Karen thanking you for getting me here... Sorry I've been such a nuisance.' She tried to keep her voice cool, not too grateful.

Jake made a gesture of impatience. 'Oh, that—that was nothing.' He looked at her critically, a slight smile lifting his lips. 'I must say you look better than the last time I saw you! How are things feeling—any pain?'

'No…a lot better, thank you.'

They stared at each other for a second in silence. Cara tried not to notice how very, very blue his eyes were, how thick and tousled his hair was over his brow. How, even now, she longed to feel his arms around her and his heart beating next to hers. She felt that familiar treacherous flutter of attraction flicker through her body, and she willed it away, pleating the sheet nervously with her fingers.

'How are things are the practice—did you manage to get a locum?' she asked at length.

'A retired doctor, Jack Stothers, has agreed to help out for a while.'

Jake put the flowers down on a table in the corner of the room, then turned round, his face grim. 'Ursula tells me you're already looking for another job, that you might move out of the area.'

Cara smiled faintly. 'Word gets round quickly. At the moment I don't feel like moving anywhere. But, of course, as things are between us, it would be better for me to move on as soon as possible…'

Her words hung starkly in the air, and Jake shook his head slowly, then sat down on the chair beside the bed. 'I didn't come here to talk about work,' he said abruptly. 'I wanted to tell you something—something I should have told you many weeks ago.'

Cara looked at him questioningly. 'What would that be?'

He ran his hand through his hair rather distractedly, so that it stood up in peaks round his head. 'Dammit,' he said huskily. 'Can't you guess?'

She shook her head in bewilderment. 'Then it's not about work?'

Jake gave a mirthless laugh. 'Don't be ridiculous! No, it's something I have much less control over than work! The truth is, Cara…' He paused for a moment, then hooked his finger under her chin, his eyes going slowly over every detail of her face. 'The truth is, I was so very, very wrong to keep backing away from you—to keep dodging any relationship. I knew it before, but I was too caught up with stupid problems of my own…and the thought that anything you felt for me might be on the rebound after Toby.'

Cara gazed at him in astonishment, then she said flatly, 'What are you talking about? You're not interested in relationships. Even if your sister hadn't told me that, I found out for myself in the end, didn't I?'

'It's not true. I mean it! There were things about my life that I thought would be unfair to burden you with—but I know I was wrong!'

Cara's looked uneasily at him. Was he just giving her the big come-on again?

'Don't give me that, Jake,' she said a little wearily. 'You don't have to make it up with me just because I've been ill, you know. I'm a big girl, I can look after myself!' She gave a wry smile. 'I've had to get over worse things than our little misunderstanding, you know! My life with Toby wasn't exactly a bed of roses.'

'So you hadn't really got over him when you came back here?' A careworn, sad expression flitted across Jake's face.

Cara shrugged. 'Actually, getting over Toby was easy when I found out what he'd done to me…and who he'd done it with!'

Jake looked at her sharply. 'A best friend—someone you knew?'

Cara hugged her arms round her body as if trying to press away the horrible image that leapt into her mind. 'You're right,' she said quietly. 'It was someone I knew, all right. It was Angela, my dear stepmother! They'd been having an affair for some time, but I only discovered it when I actually found them making love in the flat when I came in with Dan one afternoon.' She smiled grimly. 'Funny, isn't it? One woman managing to destroy two relationships—mine and my father's!'

Jake stared at her in horror. 'I'm so sorry,' he said in a low voice. 'I had no idea. And so your trust in men has been rather dented, then?'

'I told you, I've put Toby behind me and I hope I've learnt to be more discerning. That's why I don't want you to feel any sense of obligation to me because I've been ill. I can carry on with my life very well without you, Jake!'

Jake sprang up from his chair with a groan of impatience, then spun round to look at her again, his fists clenched against his sides.

'For goodness' sake, your illness may have kicked me into action, but can't you understand what I'm trying to say? I love you, dammit, and I have done for a long time!'

He knelt by the bed, his strong hands taking hers and gripping them hard, his eyes pleading. 'Sweetheart, you've got to believe me! I fell for you almost as soon as I met you—at the hogmanay dance it was, when you looked so fantastic. But I had obligations to fulfil. I thought it would be wrong to burden you with my concerns. You had responsibilities of your own—why should I add to them?'

Cara felt her heart begin to pound in her ears. Had she heard aright? Had Jake just said he loved her?

'I—I don't understand,' she stammered. 'How can you love me?' Then with more spirit, she added, 'You had a funny way of showing it!'

'I told you, I felt with my background I wasn't a suitable candidate for a lasting relationship. I tried to stop myself before it was too late.'

'So what was this obligation, this worry?'

Jake lowered his head for a moment and sighed. 'I told you that I care for Ursula very much, that I feel I owe her a lot—everything really. What I didn't tell you was that Ursula has been obsessively possessive of me for many years…so much so that for a time she didn't want me even to go to work. I was sure that if you and I got together she would make life very difficult for you. Jealousy can be a terrible and destructive thing—in Ursula it was frightening.'

'That's very sad,' whispered Cara. 'What made her so dependent?'

'A complete lack of confidence—and partly because she felt inadequate socially. I told you the mugging had changed her character. She never used to be like this.'

'Then why didn't you tell me before?'

'Because,' said Jake simply, 'I knew you were too kind and loving a person not to take on my sister. But I felt I couldn't let you carry that burden—it was my problem.'

'And what's changed your mind?' Cara's clear grey eyes gazed at him, slightly puzzled, although a sudden little ripple of excitement had started to gather strength somewhere in the pit of her stomach, as if what he was saying might just be true!

He smiled ruefully at her. 'A combination of things, I suppose. An old friend came into the surgery and reminded me how time passes, and then I realised that if anything had happened to you...' His voice was husky. 'I'd have lost you for ever...'

Cara's head whirled like the colours in a kaleidoscope. She felt confused, bewildered by the chain of events. 'But what about Ursula now. Have you told her how you feel...about me?'

Jake shook his head. 'I haven't, but I feel she's much more positive than she was—she's suddenly come out of her shell. She's become really interested in helping to organise the hospital art exhibition—and also,' he said with a twinkle, 'she seems to have fallen very heavily for little Dan! She's seen him once or twice when he's been to visit you and she's been here with her paintings—they have quite a rapport! Somehow I don't think she'd object at all to being more closely connected to him!'

He held her face between his hands. 'I'm beginning to realise that I only have one life, Cara. I can't...won't let you go. I need you more than my sister needs me,' he added softly. 'For heaven's sake, tell me I have a chance, sweetheart.'

There was a wonderful tenderness in the look he gave her, and all at once the ripple of excitement inside her became a torrent. 'I don't know what to say,' she whispered. 'I've made a fool of myself once before, allowed sweet talk to sway my judgement...'

'But do you love me?' persisted Jake, his elbows supporting him on either side of her. His face was so close to hers, those eyes so penetrating, willing her to confess that she loved him with all her heart.

Cara closed her eyes for a second. Was this just a wonderful dream, or was it real? It had happened so quickly. Ten minutes ago she'd been so sad, and now she was filled with the most delicious happiness.

She looked up into his eyes and smiled. 'I must be mad,' she whispered, 'but I guess I do...'

Jake pushed her back against the pillows, and covered her mouth with his in a lingering sweet kiss. She wound her arms about him and pressed herself to his hard chest.

'We shouldn't be doing this in here,' she whispered.

'Nonsense,' he said, lifting his mouth from hers for a second. 'This is what I prescribe for all my patients—tender loving care from someone you love!' He kissed her forehead lightly. 'I want to look after you, my darling, for the rest of my life!'

The nurse who'd opened the door behind them smiled, then went out again quietly.

EPILOGUE

ST CUTHBERT'S huge Victorian hall, surprisingly impressive for a hospital, was filled with a chattering crowd of people crowded into every available space. Round the walls paintings had been hung and on a makeshift platform at one end were myriad lights and a television camera, with a microphone dangling from loops in the ceiling. Cara swept a glance round the scene in disbelief. Only a few weeks ago the idea had been put forward to raise money—and now nearly the whole community seemed to be here!

'I must say St Cuth's doesn't look much like a hospital at the moment—certainly not with all this crowd knocking back the champagne,' observed Jake with a grin. 'They've really transformed the old place—I often thought it was a pity this magnificent space wasn't really used for anything productive.'

'It's a fantastic place for an art exhibition,' agreed Cara, sipping her drink. 'And Ursula's paintings are set off to such advantage. I think she's going to make a real mark for herself.'

Jake looked down at her with a tender smile. 'And she's got you to thank for that, I know…'

Cara opened her mouth to protest, and he put his hand up to stop her. 'No use pretending you had nothing to do with her being asked to contribute—Peter Dunne let the cat out of the bag earlier and told me it had all been your idea! Why the big secret anyway about it being your project?'

Cara looked at him from under her lashes, her lips curving in a little smile. 'You may remember that you and I had a slight cooling-off period not so long ago...'

'So you were trying to keep well away from me, is that it?' Jake gave a low chuckle, and slipped his arm round Cara's shoulders. 'What a fool I was to let that happen,' he murmured, then he tilted her head and brushed her lips with his.

'Not here, Jake—not in front of the whole of Ballranoch!' said Cara, suppressing a giggle.

'Why not? I want the world to know I've managed to catch the most wonderful girl in the world!'

It was a heady feeling, thought Cara, looking up at Jake's tall figure and his blue eyes gazing down at hers. She felt her heart was ready to burst with happiness, something she'd thought she'd never feel again. She could hardly believe that her future had changed so dramatically from a bleak outlook of being alone with Dan once more to one of excitement and planning a future for the three of them!

She gazed round the hall and felt her throat constrict as she saw two figures walking hand and hand in front of her—one old and stooped, one very small and chubby. At the end of last year, she reflected, her father hadn't even known he had a grandson, and now they had forged a loving relationship. Gordon had taken on a new lease of life, and he and Dan made little expeditions all over the area to farms, toy museums—anywhere Gordon thought the little boy would enjoy. That could be why her father had made such a marvellous recovery from his bypass operation, Cara thought. He had somebody he treasured to live for.

They were turning back towards her, and Dan suddenly broke free from his grandfather and raced towards Cara and Jake.

'Come and see Ursula!' he cried, hugging Cara round her knees with his arms. 'Grandpa says she's going to be on television—she's going to be famous!'

Jake bent down and swung the little boy up in his arms. 'You show me where she is, then,' he said affectionately, ruffling Dan's hair. 'We'll go and look at her pictures before they interview her.'

'It's remarkable,' said Gordon, as he strolled over with them. 'I should think Ursula's sold nearly all her paintings, and there's some chap from Edinburgh here who's trying to get her to agree to put on a major exhibition during the festival. I imagine the whole thing's raised a tidy sum for the heart unit here as well.'

Dan pointed to the corner near the stage where Ursula was, and they trooped over. It was hard to believe, reflected Cara, that this vibrant, smiling woman was the same shy, rather brusque person she'd first met. She watched Ursula's happy face, so engrossed and interested in explaining to the people milling round her paintings what she was trying to achieve and the particular technique she used. All her reticence and self-consciousness seemed to have vanished.

'You know,' whispered Jake, mirroring Cara's thoughts, 'it's almost as if the old Ursula I used to know before she was attacked has come back. She has so much more confidence. She's even mentioned having some of the cheek muscle in her face built back up—not really for the look of it so much but to make it more mobile and comfortable again.'

'That's a major breakthrough!' said Cara delightedly.

Jake's strong face suddenly relaxed into the rather rare happy smile that gave him such a boyish look at times. 'And it's all because of you, darling,' he said, putting Dan down and taking hold of Cara's hand and squeezing it. 'Ursula hasn't had time to dwell on her loneliness—she's been too busy bossing Peter around, telling him where she wants her paintings!'

Dan ran up to Ursula and tugged her skirt. 'When are you going to be on television, Ursula? Is it soon? If you hurry,' he added in a conspiratorial whisper, 'we can have lots to eat afterwards. It's all in another room—and I'm very, very hungry!'

A little ripple of laughter went round the knot of people by the stage as they watched his earnest little face looking up at hers.

'Ah, Dan!' said Ursula, holding out her hand to him and bending down to his level. 'My little helper! Shall I tell you something? I'm hungry as well. Perhaps I could get Jake to do the television bit for me, then we can all go and get down to the important thing of eating!' She looked up at Jake pleadingly. 'Please, Jake, I'm not ready yet for interviews—say a few words on my behalf!'

For a moment the old, shy expression returned to her face, and Jake smiled. 'If that's what you want me to do, sis, I will. You've come a long way in a short time!'

A tall man in glasses with a clipboard and nervous manner fluttered round them.

'And you are the artist's brother, I believe? Could you possibly come and speak for Miss Donahue? I can't persuade her to go in front of the camera at all! I'll just run over a few of the questions we'd like to put to you and then we'll go on camera.'

Jake nodded and went off with the man, and Ursula turned to Cara, her blue eyes, so like Jake's, holding Cara's for a moment.

'I...I wanted to have a word with you quietly,' she said hesitantly. 'I just wanted to say how grateful I am to you about...all this. It's the first time for many years that I've felt enthusiastic about anything.' She gave a nervous little laugh. 'You've done a lot to help me live again—but mostly I think it's been Dan that's pulled me back into the land of the living!'

Her voice faltered as if she found it hard to express her feelings, and her eyes followed the little boy as he watched the television crew organising the recording.

'You see,' she went on, 'he reminds me so much of Jake as a little boy! It's as if I had Jake back again. He was just as outspoken as Dan is now—said just what he thought! I'd got used to people treading on glass where I was concerned—frightened of offending me I suppose. It's refreshing to be spoken to like a normal human being!'

'He seems very fond of you, too, Ursula,' said Cara, feeling a rush of affection for this woman who had had to overcome so much in her life.

Ursula laughed, a happy natural sound. 'Yes, I really think he is!' She put a soft hand on Cara's arm. 'And that's why I'm so delighted as well that you and Jake have got together. It will be wonderful to feel that perhaps I can share in part of Dan's life as his auntie!'

Cara grinned. 'Jake didn't keep quiet about that for long,' she commented wryly.

'He didn't have to tell me.' Ursula smiled. 'I didn't need very great powers of perception to realise that my dear brother was head over heels in love. Once I'd tackled him, he couldn't wait to tell me the whole story!'

There was a sudden shrill whistle, and from the stage the nervous-looking man with the clipboard flapped his hands at the assembled throng. 'Ladies and gentlemen, quiet, please!' he shouted in a reedy voice. 'Our presenter, Lee Howard, is going to talk to Dr Jake Donahue about his sister's exhibition and the heart unit. Try and keep sound to a minimum while we make the recording.'

Cara grabbed Dan and held him still, and they both gazed up at Jake, dwarfing the small presenter and looking, thought Cara with pride, impossibly handsome in his dark suit and crisp white shirt.

'I believe your sister has been painting for many years, but this is her first exhibition?'

Jake nodded, and the monitor up on the wall showed him in close-up. 'When she was told about Sir Gordon Mackenzie's idea of helping the cardiac department, and the exhibition was suggested, she was persuaded to show some of her pictures. We hope and believe it's raised a lot of money for diagnostic equipment.' Jake looked over to Gordon who was standing at the side, watching the proceedings with a happy smile. 'I think it would be a good idea to ask Sir Gordon to say a few words himself...'

Gordon looked mildly surprised, but allowed himself to be shepherded onto the stage. Dan jumped up and down in excitement, pointing to the monitor. 'Grandpa's on TV!' he shouted, as Lee Howard moved in to speak to the old man.

'This must be a very proud moment for you, sir, managing to raise a lot of money for essential equipment at a hospital you've long been associated with. What are your thoughts?'

Gordon smiled. 'I'm a very happy man today. You see, a lot of nice things have happened to me recently—and today seems to be a culmination of that happiness!'

'And why is that?' asked the presenter courteously.

Gordon smiled even more broadly. 'Well, today I learned that my darling daughter, who came back to these parts after five years away, is to marry my partner in the practice, Jake Donahue! It's a very comforting thought for me to know that she and my little grandson Dan will be living around here for many years to come, and that Ursula Donahue, whose brilliant work has made today such a success, will be part of my family.'

Cara stared up at him, blinking back sudden tears of happiness. How could she ever have worried about coming back to Ballranoch? It had been the best thing she could have done!

Gordon was speaking again. 'I would very much like Cara, Dan and Ursula to join me with Jake on this platform because I believe they have all contributed in their way to this marvellous exhibition, and ultimately in helping to make St Cuthbert's a centre of cardiac excellence in the Highlands.'

He put his hand out towards Cara and Ursula. 'Come on,' he urged. 'I want you to be with me—please.'

Cara laughed. 'What do you think, then, Dan and Ursula? Perhaps we'd better make his day!'

Together they went onto the stage and Gordon drew them to him, Cara and Jake on one side, Dan in front of him and Ursula on the other side.

'And now, ladies and gentlemen,' said Gordon. 'Please, raise your glasses to a toast. To happiness at achieving our objective!' He looked at Cara directly for a moment, and with a slight tremor in his voice murmured, 'And to mending broken hearts again!'

A storm of clapping arose from the crowd assembled in the hall, and a shaft of sunlight from the large window suddenly bathed the group in a warm glow of light.

Jake looked down at Cara, his eyes dark with love and tenderness. 'I'll drink to that, sweetheart,' he said huskily, 'Every time!'

Modern Romance™
...seduction and
passion guaranteed

Tender Romance™
...love affairs that
last a lifetime

Sensual Romance™
...sassy, sexy and
seductive

Blaze
...sultry days and
steamy nights

Medical Romance™
...medical drama on
the pulse

Historical Romance™
...rich, vivid and
passionate

27 new titles every month.

*With all kinds of Romance for
every kind of mood...*

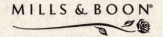

MILLS & BOON®

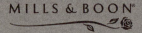

MILLS & BOON®

Medical Romance™

CHRISTMAS KNIGHT *by Meredith Webber*

As the only doctor in Testament – and a mother with a tiny baby – Kate was floundering until a knight in shining leathers drove up to her door. Local bad boy Grant Bell was now a doctor and he'd come to help. He was wonderful with Kate's patients, and with her baby – but Grant had a fiancée back in Sydney...

A MOTHER FOR HIS CHILD *by Lilian Darcy*

It had started as one night of passion – and since Will Braggett had become a partner in Maggie's medical practice it had turned into a steamy affair. As a single dad, Will's priority was his son. He wasn't ready to find him a new mother just yet. But Maggie wasn't satisfied simply being his mistress – she insisted they could only have a future if Will allowed her to get to know his child too...

THE IRRESISTIBLE DOCTOR *by Carol Wood*

Dr Alex Trent loves her new job as GP in a busy country practice. But combining motherhood and a busy career is a challenge, and Alex has no room for a man in her life – until Dr Daniel Hayward explodes onto the scene! Nine years ago their intense relationship collapsed – now Daniel's greatest desire is to reclaim Alex – this time as his wife!

On sale 1st November 2002

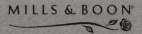

MILLS & BOON®

Medical Romance™

POLICE DOCTOR *by Laura MacDonald*

Dr Adele Brooks isn't pleased about an unexpected change of boss on her first day at Stourborne Abbas surgery – and GP and local police surgeon Casey is even less delighted about being landed with a trainee. But soon the challenges of their police work bring them closer together, and Adele has to fight the incredible attraction between them...

EMERGENCY IN MATERNITY *by Fiona McArthur*

CEO Noah Masters may be drop-dead gorgeous but surely nursing supervisor Cate Forrest can't be attracted to the man who's threatening her beloved maternity ward? But when an emergency strikes Cate and Noah are forced to work together – and they quickly realise they have feelings too powerful to be ignored...

A BABY OF HER OWN *by Kate Hardy*

Jodie Price spends Christmas in bed with her broodingly good-looking boss consultant paediatrician Sam Taylor. It seems to be the start of something special – until Sam tells her he's infertile. Sam knows Jodie wants a baby of her own. Will Jodie's need for a child be greater than her love for Sam?

On sale 1st November 2002

Available at most branches of WH Smith, Tesco, Martins, Borders, Eason, Sainsbury's and all good paperback bookshops.

Don't miss *Book Three* of this BRAND-NEW 12 book collection 'Bachelor Auction'.

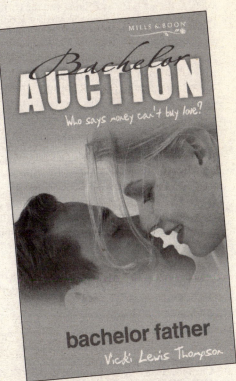

Who says money can't buy love?

On sale 1st November

2 FREE

books and a surprise gift!

We would like to take this opportunity to thank you for reading this Mills & Boon® book by offering you the chance to take TWO more specially selected titles from the Medical Romance™ series absolutely FREE! We're also making this offer to introduce you to the benefits of the Reader Service™—

- ★ FREE home delivery
- ★ FREE gifts and competitions
- ★ FREE monthly Newsletter
- ★ Exclusive Reader Service discount
- ★ Books available before they're in the shops

Accepting these FREE books and gift places you under no obligation to buy, you may cancel at any time, even after receiving your free shipment. Simply complete your details below and return the entire page to the address below. *You don't even need a stamp!*

YES! Please send me 2 free Medical Romance books and a surprise gift. I understand that unless you hear from me, I will receive 4 superb new titles every month for just £2.55 each, postage and packing free. I am under no obligation to purchase any books and may cancel my subscription at any time. The free books and gift will be mine to keep in any case.

M2ZEA

Ms/Mrs/Miss/Mr ....Initials.....................................
                                                          BLOCK CAPITALS PLEASE

Surname ....

Address ....

....

....Postcode.................................

Send this whole page to:
UK: FREEPOST CN81, Croydon, CR9 3WZ
EIRE: PO Box 4546, Kilcock, County Kildare (stamp required)